Snow from a Distant Sky

Ben Van Dongen

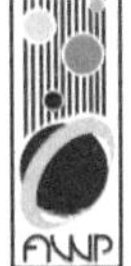

For the
Writing Wrecking
Crew
Thanks for all the
support and
encouragment

Snow from a Distant Sky

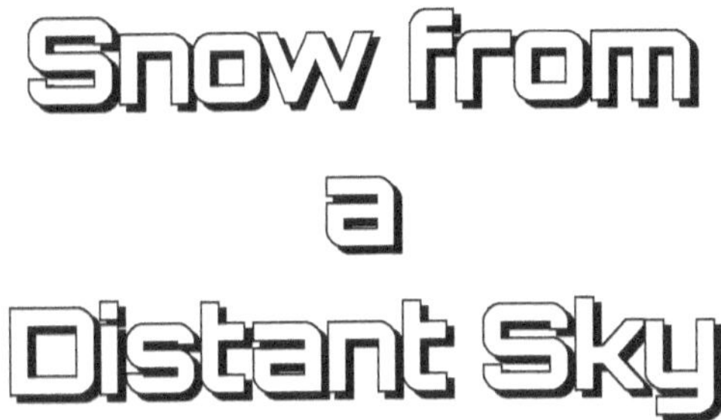

The Synthetic Albatross Series
Book Five

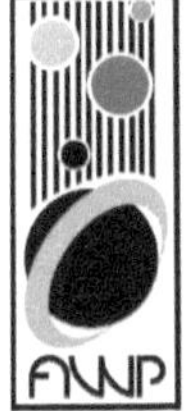

ONE
The Forest of Frozen Trees

Thomas huddled against a tall, thin tree. Relentless gusts of wind pelted him with icy snow. The clearing, nearly the same size as the basketball court he was on a moment before, was surrounded by the gaunt trees. They were bare and covered in frost but so numerous that he could only see a metre into the dead-looking woods.

The frozen snow in the glade was stained red with the blood of the monstrous creatures. They were large with wide, slumped shoulders. Their furry torsos were so big that their legs looked spindly. Thomas counted twenty-six bodies. When they had been standing and fighting they were a head taller than he was, but they were ruthlessly cut down by the robed figure.

Before the last creature succumbed to its wounds, it managed to strike down the powerful being.

When Thomas first passed through the portal to the freezing world, he backed away from the maelstrom, running into the tree. With the fighting over and no survivors, he continued to shrink against the bitter cold. The world he came from was in the midst of a suburban summer. His t-shirt and shorts let the frigid wind steal away his body heat. The yellow gem dangling around his neck seemed to hold on to the cold and push it into his skin.

Teeth chattering, his extremities going numb, Thomas forced himself to stand. He searched for the portal he'd come through. In his world, the shimmering patch in the air started as a faint distortion.

Like a shard of broken glass, it had been hard to pick out, but the world around it was refracted just enough to look out of place. It had grown, and as it did, the wintery scene expanded inside of it.

Before he could tell where the distortion ended he was inside of it, desperate to not be seen by the creatures or by the robed figure who threw fire and lightning at the attacking foes. The flashes of energy that erupted from the being had been brilliant in the dim light of the cold glade. The rift shrunk, closing off his view of the park and his high school, until he couldn't see them in the blowing snow.

On shaking legs, Thomas pushed farther into the forest. He held himself with one arm and swiped at the snow filled air with the other, desperate to find a way home.

He looked behind him and could barely see the clearing through the mass of frail trees. Changing his mind, he hurried back to it.

Closing his eyes, he fought the urge to crouch again. To lie down and rest. To let the cold and the snow cover him the way it was building up on the bodies of the monstrosities. He shook his head and trudged to the first creature. It lay on its side. Blood no longer poured from its wounds. Its furry shoulders were scorched from a fiery blast. Frost grew so quickly over the body that Thomas watched it happen in real time.

With a wince, he shook the thing. It didn't move, so he searched it. He shoved its massive shoulder and managed to roll the creature onto its back. The lumpy head flopped back and revealed a person. He was coated in black ooze, like tar, that stuck to Thomas' hands. The beastly visage was a costume.

Reaching in farther, he searched the man but found nothing. The only thing the man carried was the club that was already mostly covered in snow. Checking the next closest body, Thomas found the same, except the person inside the suit was a woman. He closed his eyes when he searched her tar-covered body, but he came up empty.

He considered putting on one of their outfits,

but the insides were as coated in goo as the bodies and the amount already on his hands was making it hard to move them in the cold.

Skipping the other bodies, he went to the robed figure. The robe itself was thin and coarse, like burlap, but it was better than the bulky, tar-coated costumes the others wore. Thomas pulled the robe off easily and slipped his arms into the sleeves. The garment was several sizes too large, but he wrapped it tightly around him. It managed to block the fierce wind.

He quickly warmed up. His teeth still clattered and his fingers and toes were still numb, but he managed to stop shaking. Pulling up the oversized hood, he looked the body over. The man who had been wearing the robe was old. His hair was white and thin and his eyebrows were bushy with long black strands that stood out against the wispy white. Deep wrinkles around his mouth made the man look angry, even in death. There was no blood, but Thomas could see where he had been struck in the head. The point of impact was slightly dented and the skin around it was black and blue. There was a large scar that came out from behind his ear. The colder the body got, the more the scar stood out against it.

The man was naked except for his sandaled feet. Thomas didn't want to believe it, but he figured the man must have had some kind of magic to be able to create fire and lightning.

Thomas had been shocked when he saw the monsters, but his uncle was a traveller who told him stories of all the strange animals that he had seen around the globe. If he really was in another world, what looked like a monster to him could easily be just an animal he had never seen before. The fact that they had turned out to be people in costume didn't change his situation.

Another thing his uncle had told him was that to people who didn't know better, science might as well be magic. When he saw the robed man create fire, he assumed it was done with some gadget. But the only thing the man had was the robe.

Standing, Thomas checked the pockets at his sides. They were deep, but empty. As he pulled his hands out, he noticed that the sleeves weren't as long as they had been. They still covered his hands, but instead of extending far beyond them, his fingertips poked out of the sleeves.

The hem at his feet brushed the snow-covered ground instead of bunching up in a pile. His fingers and toes were stiff, but the feeling was coming back, along with a dull ache.

"I don't know what you are—were, but this robe is something magical," he said to the dead man.

There is nothing magical about a piece of fabric. The

voice sounded like a whisper, but Thomas could clearly hear it over the wind. He spun in a circle, trying to find the speaker, but all he saw were the dead bodies and spindly trees.

TWO
A Shadow

Hesitantly, Thomas looked down at the body at his feet. The naked man who he had taken the robe from was motionless. His skin looked bluish.

Squinting, Thomas tried to adjust to the dim light in the snow-blanketed glade. He thought it was getting darker, as if the sun were setting, but the world he came from was in midafternoon.

Have you given up looking for me? the voice asked.

As he stared into the nearby tree line, a shadow fell over him. The growing warmth from the robe slipped away. Thomas looked up, expecting to see a large, black bird or some other terrifying creature, but there was just the shadow. It hung in the air above him, an indistinct shape with hazy boundaries like the shimmering portal.

Retreating from the amorphous darkness, Thomas tripped on a body and fell to the ground with a crunch. The snow softened the impact, but the layer of ice on top of it left jagged edges around the hole.

The shadow followed as if it were tethered to him.

"I didn't do this," Thomas said, looking at the body at his feet.

I know that. The words seemed to form inside his head. It was like he was thinking them, but they were foreign. *I did it.*

Thomas glanced at the naked man.

Yes. It was on his behalf. Though, now he is dead, as are my obligations.

Thomas stared at the shadow and angled his head towards where he'd entered the clearing, but the hood of the cloak cut off his peripheral vision.

Looking for a way out? the shadow asked.

Nodding, Thomas scooted back, carving a trench in the snow.

The shadow stuck with him. *I am not dangerous. Though I am capable of destruction.*

"I want to go home." Thomas blurted out the words and felt like a child for saying them. He thought about his parents and how long it would take before they realized he was missing.

As do we all. I'm afraid that the doorway you entered was fleeting and has gone. It is the way of these things. The chances that you had even run into one were immeasurable.

The shadow made a sound like cold laughter. *You are unlikely to stumble across another in your lifetime, even with that curious item around your neck.*

At the mention of the necklace, Thomas pulled it out from under his shirt. The spot where the yellow gem had sat against his skin was numb. The dark metal chain was freezing in his hand. He stared at the rectangular jewel. It caught the fading light and looked like it was glowing.

Yes, the shadow said. *A marvelous item. May I ask, from where did you get it?*

Thomas swallowed. "My uncle. He gave it to me for my birthday."

And he found it in your world?

"I think so." Thomas gripped the chain tightly, his hand to his chest.

Do not worry. I have no reason to take it from you, but there are some who would. It is a rare item, valuable in the right hands.

Sitting upright, Thomas leaned towards the shadow, but it kept the same distance from him. "Can I use it to get home?"

Could it assist you in finding another portal? Yes. That is not to say it would be easy.

"It started to glow." Thomas looked down at the snow he had churned up. "I was in my room doing summer homework, and the edge of it glowed. When I picked it up, it pointed me towards the park.

Like a radar or something."

And you saw the shimmer. The portal opened and you got too close. A pity.

Thomas forced himself to look at the shadow again. "Why?"

You were too eager or too stupid to keep your distance and you trapped yourself on an inhospitable world.

"I'm not stupid." Gritting his teeth, Thomas stood.

The shadow moved with him. *That was inconsiderate of me. Ignorant may have been a more appropriate word. Either way, you are in a predicament. It was smart of you to don the cloak. It will keep you much more comfortable than the horrid costumes of those primitives. It does come with a hitch, however.*

"What's that?" Thomas tucked the necklace back under his shirt and pulled the robe tighter around him.

I am bound to the cloak, which means I am stuck with you.

Glancing at the naked body, Thomas smirked. "Would it be better to be stuck with the dead man?"

Certainly not. I was forced to do his bidding for far too long. He called himself a wizard and used me to help manifest those parlor tricks.

Thomas thought of the fire and lightning. "You did that?"

I made it possible.

"But he forced you?"

I will not say that showing my ability was completely unpleasant, but I have little reason to dominate a tribe of savages.

"How did he force you to do anything?" Thomas went back to the man. He was old, but looked like he had been strong. Otherwise, he seemed unremarkable, especially with snow piling up around his naked body.

I will not fall for such an obvious ploy.

Thomas put up his hands. "I didn't mean… It's just surprising."

A likely response. My time working with this lesser being is over and while I have no intention of entering into a contract with you, we could be of some use to each other.

"Could you help me get home?"

Unlikely, but I am probably your best option in that respect. The shadow seemed to stare at him. *You are trapped on a hostile planet and frankly, you are underdressed. I am inexorably tied to the cloak and have no means of locomotion. If we were to work together, we would have a chance to both get what we want.*

Thomas furrowed his brow. "Isn't that basically a contract?"

The debate of semantics is unworthy of my attention. Though, for the sake of brevity, a contract is legally binding, or in this case fundamentally so. What I'm proposing is a simple agreement to assist each other for mutual benefit. You could always take the robe off and freeze to death in this dying forest.

"I suppose it makes sense. Though, all I really want is to go home." Thomas grimaced.

What you want is irrelevant in the face of reality. Have you ever heard of Maslow? The Hierarchy of Needs?

"No."

How old are you?

Thomas sneered at the shadow. "Sixteen."

What a poor world you must come from that your education is so inadequate. The point I am trying to make is that you face the threat of death, which, in this instance, is more pressing than your desire to return home. Worry about what is in front of you first.

"Okay. So, I help you get out of here and you help me stay alive so that I can eventually find a way home." Crossing his arms, Thomas shifted his weight to one leg.

You are not so simple after all.

"So, what do you want?"

To get out of this clearing in the middle of the forest, obviously.

Thomas shook his head. "After that. Where do you want to go and why?"

An important question for once. I have no need to be in any one specific place, but not being here would be preferable. Ultimately, I suppose I would like to find more of my kind. But for now, I will be content with leaving here. In return, you may use my robe for protection and I shall offer you guidance. Do we have a deal?

Thomas hesitated. He ran through what the shadow had said, looking for loopholes. "Deal."

Excellent. I suppose the first thing we should do is get away from this mess before someone comes along and blames you for it. Head north.

"Which way is that?" Thomas turned in a circle, scanning the identical tree line on all sides of him.

Do you know which way north was in your world?

"Yeah."

It will be the same here.

Looking back to where he had first entered the clearing, Thomas thought about the basketball court, which was on the south side of the school. Turning back to where the naked man was lying, he headed into the forest.

Snow from a Distant Sky

14

THREE
A Rogue

Thomas walked in as straight a line as he could through the dense forest of thin trees. The wind constantly blew snow through the woods in gusts. He kept the hood up on the robe and felt his way forward with outstretched arms. Even when he reached the edge of the woods and the density of trees thinned, the light was dim and grey.

His feet dragged, making channels through the snow with each step. At the deepest, it reached his knees, though the cloak managed to ward off the worst of the cold. Staggering out of the forest, he stopped and clutched at his rumbling stomach.

"Is there somewhere I can find food?" he asked the shadow.

The dark shape had sunk back into the brown fabric of the cloak, dissipating across the material. *If you were clever enough, you could potentially catch a wild animal, but there are few and they are wary of humans.*

"I've been walking for hours and I'm starving." Thomas trudged through a snow bank.

You could always fill your belly with ice, but that would ultimately make you more hungry in the long run.

"If I don't find something to eat soon, I won't be able to carry you much farther." Thomas stopped and looked across the dull horizon. He could see the tree line continue to his right. It curved back in front of him in the distance like the shore of a lake.

To his left was open land. The wind blew fiercely across the field, carrying more stinging snow with it. Three small circles in the sky shone meekly, as if they were on the verge of burning out. The yellow disc was brightest, but it was the smallest. The other two sources of light were red, tinting the white landscape.

This world is harsh, the shadow said.

Thomas huffed. Reaching down, he scooped up a handful of the snow at his knee and took a bite. It crunched in his mouth and sent a spike of pain behind his eyes.

Slowly or you will bring your core temperature down.

Wincing, Thomas nodded. "I thought it was dusk back at the clearing. Or at least, I figured it would get brighter when we got out of the woods." He stared at the red orbs low in the sky. "You'd think with three suns this place would be warmer, too."

Not three suns, the shadow said. *Two suns and a planet, though not for long.*

"Whatever." Thomas felt the snow in his belly. It chilled his insides and did nothing for the hunger pangs. "How much farther do I have?"

Until?

"We come across something. I find food?"

How would I know?

Thomas looked down at the robe. "I thought you were going to guide me."

This is a large and empty world. I do not have it memorized, nor do I know what it is you're looking for.

"You told me I wasn't going home any time soon, so I'll settle for something to eat." Clenching the sleeve in his hand, Thomas kicked at the snow around his legs.

You may want to look for a settlement, since hunting is beyond your current abilities.

"You told me to go north."

It was the safest route away from your current position. The man who previously wore the cloak terrorized the local population. It would be unwise for you to run into that tribe.

"So, you don't know where we're going?" Thomas wavered on his feet and dropped to his butt, sinking into the drift.

We are going north. The shadow grumbled for a moment. *You should not sit. It will get harder and harder to stand.*

With a huff, Thomas got to his feet, packing down more of the snow and coating his tar covered hands in the icy particles. Though, when the sleeves covered them, the ice melted quickly, but the robe didn't get wet. He rubbed the material between a thumb and forefinger, but it just felt like coarse fabric.

"How far would I have to go to get somewhere warmer?" he asked.

There is nowhere warmer. Not significantly and not within walking distance.

Frowning, Thomas trudged forward. "This world sucks."

You have no idea.

Keeping to the left, Thomas avoided going back into the forest, but he didn't wander far from the trees. He thought that if he had to sleep before finding shelter, he would rather do it next to a tree than out in the open.

He felt a pit in his already pained stomach at the thought of leaving the woods behind. As if he would become untethered in the blank canvas of the open landscape. Through the gusts of snow, he spotted a line of objects in the distance. They were hollow towers of crisscrossing steel, narrow in the middle with triangular arms at the top.

The things were familiar, but he wasn't sure why.

He pointed to them. "What are those?"

Remnants of the past.

Slumping his shoulders, he crossed his arms against the growing cold. The three balls in the sky were getting closer to the horizon. "That's not a helpful answer."

The shadow didn't reply, so Thomas headed towards the closest one. As they got bigger, he noticed more detail. Some of them were on an angle, as if the wind or snow had shoved them over. Then, he spotted the thick cables that dangled from a few of the extended arms and stopped his approach.

"Are those hydro towers?" The pit in Thomas' stomach grew as the pangs faded.

They would have been called that at one time. Or electrical pylons.

"How deep is the snow?" Thomas stared at the partially buried towers.

It varies, but here the snow is approximately twenty metres deep.

Thomas took a deep, cold breath. "Where am I?"

I do not know the name of the exact county, but this was known as North America, once.

"This is Earth?" Fighting tears, Thomas felt his fatigue weighing him down.

Not your Earth, if that is bothering you. There are infinite Earths and you stumbled from yours to this one. Lucky boy.

Thomas closed his eyes as the few tears that escaped clung to his cheeks, threatening to freeze. "What happened?"

The brighter of the red orbs in the sky is an intergalactic star. A wanderer. It got too close to this Earth and knocked it out of orbit. The coward is running away, its direction changed by the sun, which looks like it is shrinking since this planet is drifting farther from it.

"And the other red disk?"

Is Mars. The Earth has become what is known as a rogue planet. It will slip deeper into the solar system, getting colder and colder, and will eventually sail off into empty space, a lifeless ball of ice and rock.

Thomas retched. He spat gobs of saliva and stomach acid into the snow at his feet and wiped his mouth with the back of his hand.

That will not help your hunger.

Before he could answer, Thomas heard a crunch behind him. He turned as something pounced, pushing him into his own vomit.

A huge shaggy maw pressed into his face.

The figure on top of him sat up. Under the chin of the beast, he spotted the eyes of a person. They smaller than the ones he had seen back in the clearing, but was strong enough to keep Thomas pinned.

"Give up, wizard." The high-pitched voice was quiet but firm.

Thomas' teeth chattered again. "I'm not a wizard. I—I found this robe in the forest. I was cold."

"Not a word, or I'll gag you." The figure flipped Thomas onto his stomach and tied his hands behind his back. When they finally got off of him, the person pulled on his bound wrists, forcing him to stand. Staying behind him and out of sight, they jabbed him in the back with something pointed.

"Move."

"I'm starving. I can't walk all the way back there." Thomas tried to look behind him, but as soon as his head turned, he was jabbed again.

"Walk or I'll kill you now."

You'd better do as she says, the shadow said.

Fighting another wave of nausea, Thomas started to walk back the way he'd come, noticing the light footprints of the woman next to his messy trenches.

Snow from a Distant Sky

FOUR
The Tribe

Thomas was walked back into the forest at spear-point. Any time he slowed down or stumbled, the woman would jab him in the back. He wasn't sure if she was skilled enough to cause him pain without cutting the robe, or if the robe was much more difficult to cut than it looked.

When they passed through the clearing where he first arrived, he saw blood-stained divots in the snow, but the bodies of the warriors were gone. The naked man was still lying where Thomas had left him. One side of the body was covered in snow, and Thomas guessed it wouldn't be long before all evidence of the battle would be buried.

Dragging his feet, his shoe caught on a tree root and he fell to his knees. Wincing, Thomas braced for the point of the spear in his back.

"Get up." Instead of the point, the woman

tapped him with the butt end of the spear. "We have a long way to go."

Thomas tried to stand, slipped, and with his hands bound, fell face first into the crunchy snow. Extricating himself, he sat on his haunches. "I'm starving."

There was a pause and he felt the urge to look behind him. Before he could turn his head, something fell next to him.

It was a cloth-wrapped bundle about the size of an orange.

"Take it, you can eat on the move. It'll get dark soon." With a quick swipe, the woman cut his bonds.

Like a hungry animal, Thomas snatched the bundle before it could be taken away. Standing, he unwrapped the cloth. The smell hit him through the cold numbing his nose. It was the reek of fermentation, strong and slightly sour. The pinkish-grey substance was hard and there was a thin layer of slime coating the exterior, like meat left in the fridge too long.

He felt the spear in his back again, and he shuffled forward. Within a few steps hunger won him over and he took a bite.

The taste of rot overwhelmed him and he gagged, but he was too scared to spit the food out and risk the wrath of the woman forcing him to march. Chewing as little as possible, he swallowed.

The tough, slimy texture slide easily into his stomach. He waited a long time before taking another bite, but the second one came much easier and he finished the lump of what he hoped was jerky.

The taste clung to his tongue. As the food digested, he was less fatigued, though his legs and feet were still cold and sore.

He stuffed the cloth into his pocket. "Thank you," he said, facing forward.

The woman grunted.

They continued, the best that Thomas could tell, south from the glade. The forest got darker, the waning light becoming distinctly red. He couldn't see the suns or Mars through the skinny trees, but he figured the sun he knew was setting and the others were following close behind.

The temperature dropped rapidly, the cold wind breaking through the magic of the robe. Thomas shivered.

He felt a hand on his back and flinched. The shape of the woman wearing the oversized beast costume was beside him, partially blocked by his hood.

"We have to hurry. It's going to start to freeze soon." She urged him on, continuing to push his back.

"This isn't freezing?" Thomas risked a glance. He saw her eyes under the creature's maw on top of her head. They were bright against her tar-covered face. In the waning, reddish light, her irises looked yellow. She was shorter than he was, her head reaching his shoulder, though the top of her outfit loomed over him.

Thomas picked up his feet, matching her pace. Even without his hands tied behind his back, he struggled to keep his balance in the deep snow. He used the trees for support, but some of them weren't sturdy and leaned away from his touch with a groan.

"Be careful, the forest is fragile." The woman gave him a shove and kept pushing him with the shaft of the spear.

The light faded, and somehow, the temperature kept dropping. The numbness that the cloak had been keeping at bay crept into Thomas' bones. His face started to sting and his wet socks hardened.

"Almost there." The woman slowed. Slinging the spear over her back, she pulled a satchel around to her side. She took out a stick and something Thomas couldn't make out in the darkness. Shoving the stick into her armpit, she smashed the things in her hands together and made a spark. The stick caught quickly.

She held the torch out in front of them as she put the stones, or flint, back in her bag.

With her spear away, Thomas considered running. Then, he thought about the temperature and his lack of food or shelter and put the thought out of his mind. He would be better off being a prisoner than freezing to death in the night. He guessed that she wouldn't have any trouble catching him, either. Especially since she had sneaked up on him so easily back at the hydro towers.

The woman grabbed Thomas' sleeve and waved the torch back and forth.

Strangely, the fire didn't help him see where they were going. The immediate surroundings were cast in flickering light, but the forest beyond the reach of the torch was plunged into complete darkness.

In the distance, he spotted another moving torch through the spindly trees. Then several more came to life, illuminating a path forward.

He and the woman emerged from the woods into a wide-open space that sloped gradually down to their left. He could make out the shape of a partially collapsed building, but not much else in the blowing snow and darkness.

The lights came closer as the woman pulled him towards the structure. The other torch wielders wore similar animal hoods, though most of them looked much larger than the woman. One of them handed a torch off to another and hurried ahead of the group.

"Cutting it close, again," the man said.

"I got the job done."

The woman continued to a set of doors that

were opened from inside by people wearing animal pelts, but without the hood, or tarred skin.

Inside was dark except for the torches. In the dancing light, Thomas made out the dilapidated state of the hallway. Snow made it inside through holes in the roof and walls, accompanied by howling wind, but it was slightly warmer.

The woman shouldered her way through another door that creaked loudly as it opened. On the other side was a set of stairs going down.

The man who had approached her outside caught up and grabbed her by the shoulder.

"You can't bring him down. It's not safe," he said. His hand looked massive on her fur covered arm.

"Should we leave him outside? How about up here, where he can sit and plan alone, if he doesn't freeze to death." Pulling free from the man's grip, still holding on to Thomas, she descended the stairs, the torch in her hand failing to light the way.

FIVE
What Remains

The wide staircase led down, turning back on itself. At the bottom was another hallway with closed doors along both walls. At the end was an illuminated exit sign over a set of double doors. The woman led Thomas to the sign and plunged her torch into a barrel of melting snow against the wall.

The steel container was dented in the middle and most of the paint had given way to rust. Thomas thought it looked a lot like the large trash cans from the park near his house. Before he could take a closer look at the worn words on the dented barrel, he was pushed through the doors.

Thomas heard the rumble of a generator and saw the machine at the edge of a spotlight in the back corner of the room. The light wavered with the sound of the struggling motor. A waft of acrid fumes tainted the enclosed space.

The rest of the room was dark, but he could make out a few tables with attached benches. He knew that they were designed to fold up and roll out of the way because they were the same kind of cafeteria tables his high school used. He got a close up view of the scarred surface of the nearest one when the woman shoved him into it and held his head down.

Thomas heard footsteps come into the room and the voice of the man who had chastised the woman twice already.

"What's your plan, Teacup?"

"Call the Chief," she said. "I don't think this one is a wizard, so wake the Healer, too." The pressure of her hand on Thomas' head was steady. "I think he may have come from another world."

"Ridiculous," the man said.

"The attack against the wizard was a success, though we lost the entire raiding party. The clearing was a mess of footprints, but there was a set that seemed to appear at the edge and exited the grove heading north. I followed them and caught this one. He didn't even struggle. He's no wizard."

"That doesn't mean he's from another world."

"Look at his shoes." The woman reached down and grabbed Thomas by the ankle, holding his foot in the air.

Thomas saw the glow of a torch come into view.

"Go get the Chief and Healer," the man said to someone out of sight and the torch glow retreated.

The woman let go of Thomas and his foot dropped to the floor. More spotlights came on and the generator protested with the sustained squeal of a slipping belt. Thomas saw a wide alcove in the back of the room and noticed marks on the wall where a stage may have once been. He guessed in the icy world, the wood was more valuable as something to burn. The paint on the walls was peeling and flaking off, leaving stained cinder block.

Before he could speculate further, more people arrived.

"What is so important that you had to wake me in the middle of the night, Roman?" a woman asked. She stopped next to the table and Thomas could see her long, dark hair against a tattered blue housecoat.

"Chief," the man said. "Teacup caught this man fleeing the battle against the wizard and brought him here."

Thomas thought he had misheard the man when he first called the woman Teacup.

"Is that true?" the Chief asked.

"Yes, ma'am," Teacup said. "I think he's a traveller."

"He's clearly a wizard," the man said.

"Or he took the robe off of the wizard when he found himself in a new world, unprepared for the cold."

"The healer can sort this out," the Chief said.

As if being announced, Thomas heard shuffling slippers and a loud yawn.

"You called for me?" The new voice was gruff and low, like a lifelong smoker.

"Please inspect this man," the Chief said.

"And what am I looking for?" The Healer came to the table. "Please remove your hand, Teacup."

Roman stepped into view. "Is that wise? He is dressed like the wizard."

"Are you blind?" The Healer asked. "This is clearly a boy."

Teacup let Thomas go and the healer pulled back the hood on the robe.

"Now, hold still, son. Don't want to startle the already tense warriors." The Healer leaned in close and tilted Thomas' head forward to expose his neck. With a dry hand, he traced a line behind Thomas' left ear, where the naked man's scar had been.

"There's no sign of implantation." Reaching back, the Healer took out a device that looked like the type of scanners couples used to register for a wedding. The Healer held it to the same spot behind Thomas' neck until there was a beep. "And I'm not detecting anything. It appears he's clean." The Healer put the scanner away and hooked a finger on the chain around Thomas' neck. Drawing out the gem, he held it up to the light and looked at it so closely that his eye almost touched it.

"Is that anything?" the Chief asked.

"May have been valuable once. It's a rock, now. Would you like me to look him over for anything else? Signs of hypothermia, maybe?"

"No. Thank you, Healer," the Chief said.

The Healer helped Thomas sit up. He had a bulbous, red nose and was bald, except for the wild strands of white hair at the sides of his head. Closing one bloodshot eye, he looked closely at Thomas with the other. "Warm that nose up, son. You don't want it to turn black and fall off."

Waving to the Chief, he turned and shuffled out of the room. Thomas noticed the man's ragged slippers were held together with twine.

No longer face-first against the table, Thomas could see the others clearly. The man the Chief called Roman had wiped the tar from his face, though there was plenty of the gooey stuff along his hairline and in his beard. He was tall, Thomas guessed more than a head taller than he was, and his thin shirt showed his muscled shoulders and arms. He hovered next to the Chief, as if he were expecting Thomas to shoot fire from his hands the way the naked man had.

The Chief was about Thomas' height. She held her head high, but she looked like she was wearing an old bathrobe she'd found in the trash. Her eyes seemed to skip over Thomas as she turned to face Teacup.

The short warrior woman was still wearing the animal head. In the wavering spotlights, it looked like a bearskin rug draped over her.

"Well." The Chief clasped her hands together. "Now that we know he's not a wizard, what do we do with him?"

"If he's a traveller, he could be helpful," Teacup said.

Roman stepped in front of Teacup, towering over her. "Travellers are a myth. No one can save us from the freezing."

"Travellers have to be presented," the Chief said. Both Roman and Teacup turned to face her. "Whether or not he can help us, he seems to be no threat for now. I'm going back to bed. We can sort it out in the morning."

"He may not be a wizard, but we have no way of knowing if he is a threat," Roman said.

"I'll watch him tonight." Teacup stared up at the larger warrior. "I'm the one who caught him and brought him here."

"That's fine by me." The Chief tilted her head to the side. "Does that satisfy you, Roman?"

"For now." The large man stomped off. Slamming the doors open, he disappeared down the dark hallway.

"Don't worry about him." The Chief glanced at both Thomas and Teacup, so he didn't know whom she was addressing. "He sees everything as a threat and that robe doesn't help."

"Would you like me to find him something else to wear?" Teacup asked.

Thomas slid off the table. "I'd prefer to, uh." He looked at the floor. "To keep it."

"It's too late for me to worry about it." The Chief headed for the doors. "Expect dirty looks from the others."

When she was gone, Teacup grabbed Thomas by the arm. "Come on."

Snow from a Distant Sky

SIX

Teacup

Teacup turned off all the spotlights except the one by the generator, dragging Thomas with her. She led him back into the hallway and through a door that led to a perpendicular corridor.

The hallway was nearly pitch-black and Thomas could only see the doors as they passed them. Teacup pulled him around several turns that he struggled to keep track of and stopped in front of a door that seemed indistinguishable from all the others.

"One sec," she whispered.

Thomas heard her rustling around in her bag, then the sound of a lock being opened. She shoved him into the room and closed the door behind her.

Still unable to see anything but vague, grey shapes, Thomas stood still until Teacup lit a candle and placed it in a holder next to the door. The tiny, flickering flame seemed bright in the narrow space.

There was a bunk at the back of the room, its metal frame bent in order to fit. A locker stood against one of the walls with a sagging coatrack next to it and a trunk on the floor. On the opposite wall was a tiny table with a single chair that took up the rest of the space.

Sloughing off the animal pelt, Teacup draped it over the coatrack. The wood protested against the weight. Opening the locker, she stuffed her bag inside and grabbed a towel that looked dirty in the candlelight. She wiped the tar from her face as she went to the table. Slinging the towel over her neck, she grabbed a basin from the floor. She placed the large, chipped bowl on the table and filled it with water from a jug.

"What's your name?"

"Tom, Thomas."

Looking over her shoulder, Teacup held the jug out to him. "Want a drink?"

"Is it clean?" Thomas reached for the bottle and felt a sticky dryness in his mouth.

"It's melted snow." Without waiting for Thomas to reply. Teacup let go of the jug and plunged her hands into the basin. She splashed the water over her head and started to scrub.

The tar and water splattered the wall and ran down her shoulders. Thomas looked away when she pulled her slick undershirt over her head. He took a big swig from the jug and winced at the icy temperature of the water inside. A sigh escaped his lips when he finished, though.

Risking a glance, Thomas saw the shape of Teacup's naked back and arms as black rivulets ran down them and dripped to the floor. He noticed the hint of her muscles under a layer of soft flesh. The waistband of her pants accentuated the curve of her hips. She looked like she was built for the cold.

A series of scars were carved into her back. He traced them with his gaze and imagined what animal or weapon could have made them.

"Done with that water?"

Thomas looked up and met her eyes. They didn't stand out as much with the tar mostly washed away, but they gleamed in the candlelight. He turned away, took another hurried sip, and then handed the bottle back to her.

She took it, but held on to his wrist. "Now he's shy."

"I'm sorry. I didn't mean to stare."

"How old did you say you were?"

"Sixteen." Thomas gazed at the face of her pelt staring back at him from the coatrack.

"If you were from this world, you'd have found a partner and had a few kids by now." Teacup let him go. "That wasn't an invitation."

"Okay."

Teacup came up behind him and Thomas froze. He could feel her warm breath on his neck, the fog visible in the faint light.

She put a hand on his back and gently moved him towards the pelt.

Walking forward with stilted steps, he stopped short of the maw of the beast. He heard splashing and looked down to see her dumping the basin into a drain in the middle of the room. The towel dangled on either side of her shoulders, blocking his view.

"So, what now?" he asked.

"Bedtime." Teacup tossed the towel towards the locker. It hit the open door with the weight of the tar and water, and plopped to the floor. She pulled down her pants and kicked off her shoes before crawling into her small cot.

"Where do I sleep?" Thomas turned in place, looking over the small room again.

"The floor, I guess." Teacup rolled onto her side and pulled a rough blanket over her bare shoulder. "And blow the candle out. They're hard to come by."

Thomas crouched to check the floor. The drain in the middle was wet, limiting his options. He blew out the candle and sat in between the locker and coat rack. Pulling up the hood on the cloak, he rested his head on the side of the locker.

That was a close call, the shadow said in his mind.

Thomas glanced around the room, but didn't see the dark shape.

"I'm still scared," he whispered.

You should be. They do not seem to think you are a wizard. They suspect you are from another world, though. Even if the Chief has doubts, she will send you to be presented. That means more time out in the cold world and who knows what sort of peril.

"You sound excited." Thomas pulled his arms out of the sleeves and rubbed his shoulders inside the cloak.

The journey is its own reward. And, the more I travel, the more likely I can find others.

"Will I be able to find a way home?"

You will have a better chance out there. This is a small settlement of stubborn people who pointlessly struggle against the growing cold.

"Where will they take me? To be presented?"

The cot creaked as Teacup shifted. "Stop talking to yourself and go to sleep! The Chief will call for us early."

There was more creaking as she settled. Thomas gritted his teeth and closed his eyes.

Snow from a Distant Sky

SEVEN
What to do with Thomas

The sound of banging woke Thomas. The impacts rang out with metallic decay hanging in the air. He opened his eyes, but the room was still dark. He sat upright and felt a sharp kink in his neck. Slipping his arms back into the sleeves of the robe, he yawned.

Another bang at the door made him flinch and he bashed his elbow into the locker.

Teacup sat up in bed, the blanket flopping off of her.

Thomas couldn't see her well in the dark room, but he still looked away.

"I'm up!" She swung her feet over the edge and stood. Stepping into the pants she had worn the day before, she pulled them up then reached for something under the bed.

It looked like a suitcase to Thomas—like something his grandparents would have taken on a trip in a propeller plane. Teacup riffled through it, pulling out another undershirt. She slipped it on and kicked the case back under the bed, the lid snapping shut as it hit the frame.

Thomas cleared his throat, hoping to remind the warrior that he was in her room.

"You okay?" she asked.

"Yeah." Thomas struggled to stand in the tight nook where he had been sleeping and almost knocked over the coat rack. His legs were stiff and his feet were so cold they hurt.

With a stretch, Teacup stepped into her boots and went to the door. "Good. We have to go meet with the Chief."

Thomas followed her into the hallway and stood to the side as she locked her door. It was slightly brighter outside her room. As they headed down the narrow corridor, Thomas noticed light from the open doorways. He spotted flickering candles, old lanterns, and a few dim flashlights in the rooms they passed. The people inside were lying on their beds, sitting at their small tables, or working out.

Some of them stopped what they were doing when they spotted him, and a few even stepped into the hallway to keep staring. He heard whispers, but couldn't make out what they were saying to each other.

When he and Teacup reached the perpendicular

hallway that he'd been down the night before, they turned towards the stairs instead of the cafeteria. They stopped at the door closest to the bottom of the stairs where a warrior stood wearing a pelt and holding a spear.

Behind them, the doors to the cafeteria were open and the spotlights on, so Thomas could see that the spear the man held was a piece of rusted fence post with a knife attached to the end. He may have been Roman. He was about the same size and had a beard, but Thomas couldn't tell through the pelt and tar.

The man stepped to the side and opened the door. "She's waiting for you."

Teacup nodded. She looked small next to the man, but her presence was similarly intimidating. Her shoulders were back and she took decisive steps, leading Thomas through the door.

The Chief was sitting at a desk with a corner broken off, leaving a rough edge of fiberboard. With the desk in the middle of the room, facing the door, there wasn't much more space. In the corner there was what looked like a child's dresser with most of the vibrant colour worn away and a rusty filing cabinet next to it. Maps and charts were tacked to the walls and a cord dangled from the ceiling plugged into a spotlight that lit the room unevenly.

The woman looked up. Glasses, with one of the

lenses missing, sat at the end of her nose. "Teacup. You brought me a sleepless night."

"I'm sorry."

In the spotlight, Thomas could make out Teacup better. She still had bits of tar behind her ears, on her neck, and at her elbows. It made her short hair stick up in odd places. What wasn't tinted black looked light brown or blond in comparison. Her tank top was stained around the collar, as if she could never really get rid of the tar.

Taking off the glasses, the Chief rubbed her eyes. "I met with the others this morning. They're up in arms. The Captain wanted me to strip you of your warrior status."

"You can't do that. I passed the test like everyone else!" Teacup clenched her fists.

The Chief put up her hand. "Hold it. I'm talking, you're listening."

Teacup dropped her chin.

"Everyone was against keeping the traveller here, if he is a traveller." Opening a drawer, the Chief pulled out a brown bottle. Twisting out the cork, she poured a clear liquid into a beat-up tin cup. Thomas could smell the alcohol from across the room. It burned his nostrils.

"The Healer was the one voice of opposition, but he doesn't get a full vote." The Chief jammed the cork back in the bottle before putting it away.

She slammed the drawer shut, then took a swig from the cup.

"You're going to take him to be presented. She can sort it out and clean up the mess however she sees fit."

Teacup took a deep breath and reset her shoulders. "I think that's the wrong decision."

"You get less of a say than the Healer. We just got rid of the wizard and we have to prepare for winter." The Chief finished her drink.

A shiver ran down Thomas' spine at the thought that the frozen wasteland outside wasn't as bad as it got.

"If I may?" Teacup stood as rigid as Thomas had the night before in her room.

Sighing, the Chief waved her hand holding the glasses. "Fine."

"I believe he is a traveller. His footprints just showed up in the clearing. He is wearing strange shoes, he wandered towards the open plains."

"He could be from the capital," the Chief said.

"Why would he put on the wizard's robes? He isn't dressed for the weather. How did he get here?" Teacup took half-a-step towards the old desk.

"I don't know. He could be the wizard in another body?"

"The Healer checked him last night. No scar."

The Chief leaned back in her chair. "Say he is a

traveller. What then?"

Teacup let her shoulders drop. "I'm not sure, but the last traveller was a hero. She led the tribe in the ruins to build the capital."

"You want him to be Chief? Make this place a new capital? Maybe lead us to war against the tribe in the ruins?"

"No." Teacup shook her head. "But there's a chance he could be helpful here. The freezing is getting worse."

Thomas shrank into the background as much as he could. The more they talked about him and the state of the rogue world, the more overwhelmed he felt.

The Chief sat forward and rested her elbows on the desk. "There's no certainty he'll be any help to anyone and if the capital finds out he is here, they may decide to just wipe us out. It's already been decided."

Teacup spun to face Thomas. "Don't you have anything to say?"

Thomas swallowed. "I am from another world. I'm pretty sure." He furrowed his brow. "But I'm just a kid. I don't know how I could help anyone. I just want to go home."

Teacup sneered at him. Thomas thought she looked hurt, like she'd just been dumped. Her face was round and her features delicate. The tar residue highlighted the hair between her eyebrows and on her upper lip, but she didn't look much older than he was. She could have been a senior at his school.

He thought she belonged in the frozen world, though. She had tracked him and caught him as easily as he could walk to the corner store. She outmatched him. The pit in his stomach that he'd felt since arriving through the portal, twisted. He felt like he'd let her down.

"This discussion is over," the Chief said.

Teacup whirled towards her, as if she wasn't finished arguing her case.

Before she could say anything else, Thomas' stomach rumbled.

The Chief stood. "Eat, gather what you need for the journey. You're taking him to be presented."

"Just me?" Teacup was back in her warrior stance.

"Do you need help?"

"No, Chief."

"Go. Be safe and get back to us as soon as you can. We'll need your help for winter preparations." The Chief gestured to the door.

Snow from a Distant Sky

EIGHT
The Most Important Meal

Teacup took Thomas back to her room. Dragging her chest from under her bed, she took out a black stained canvas backpack. She stuffed clothes into it and looked over her shoulder at him.

"There's a satchel in my locker. Get it for me."

Thomas did, shoving the wet towel out of the way of the locker door with the toe of his sneaker.

Taking it from him, Teacup transferred the two rocks, a knife, a metal bottle, and other objects he didn't recognize into the backpack and handed the satchel back. "You can use this. It's a bit beat up, but I patched it the best I could."

Teacup stood. From under her mattress she grabbed a knife, the blade thin from years of sharpening. "Take this too. It's not much, but everyone should carry a knife."

Thomas took it from her. The satchel was green,

like it had been military surplus in its first life. There were patches sewn to the sides and bottom made from a variety of fabric. Letting out the strap, he slung it over a shoulder and stuck the old knife into one of the outside pockets.

Teacup moved to the locker and continued to pack. When she finished, she tied up the opening of her bag, secured the flap over the top, and put on a sweater. Like all her clothes, the neck and sleeves were discolored. The rest of the ratty garment was crimson with holes that could have been made by moths, or more likely weapons.

Thomas didn't think moths would have survived long in the frozen world. He stood by the door, try-ing to keep out of her way. "Is there anything I can carry for you?"

"Uh?" Teacup dug through the locker. "I guess you can take the candle. Someone'll swipe it if I leave it here. There should be a flint and some rags you can take, too."

Thomas grabbed the candle and the flint that dangled from the holder. He found the tar-stained rags in a basket on the floor and jammed them into an outer pocket in order to keep the interior from getting more dirty than it already was. Remembering the cloth in his pocket, he added that to the bag too.

"We'll get food on the way out. I need more war paint, too." Teacup held an empty tin can that was coated in the remains of the black ooze. She slung the backpack over her shoulders, tying the straps together across her chest. Donning her pelt, she grabbed her spear and ushered Thomas into the hallway.

She locked the door and led him back to the cafeteria. There were more open doors in the narrow corridor and more people stared and murmured as they passed.

The cafeteria was full. All the spotlights were on, their light fluctuating with the strained sounds of the generator.

A row of filthy folding tables was lined up along one wall with enough space behind for people to serve what food there was. There was a foul smell from the tables, but people lined up, holding their plates, bowls, and whatever else they had, to receive their portions. Thomas saw a woman using a hubcap as a dish.

The cafeteria-style tables were full. People ate and chatted. The tone was more upbeat than Thomas expected. One of the tables erupted in laughter and the joke spread around the room, the mirth following in its wake.

Teacup led him to the end of the row of tables, cutting off several people. A man wearing a tar-stained shirt protested, slamming his cracked plate onto the table.

"No cuts!" he yelled, spittle flying from his lips.

Pushing Thomas aside, Teacup stepped up to the larger warrior. "Move me." She kept her spear-point in the air, but her grip tightened.

The man grumbled something under his breath and the woman behind him put her hand on his shoulder. "He didn't mean nothing by it. Did you, Storm?"

Shrugging off the hand, the man left his plate and walked away. "It's rude."

Teacup nodded to the woman, then went back to the end of the table. The man standing on the other side was short, his back hunched. He had wiry hair mostly covered in a yellowed bandana and a shirt that was two sizes too large, like he'd lost a lot of weight.

"What'ch you need, Cup?" He held a large serving spoon over a tray of something that looked a little like ground beef to Thomas, but the little bits were too big and too grey.

"I have to take this guy to the capital. I need rations."

"So this—the guy, huh?" The server dropped the spoon into the tray and Thomas thought he saw the food move. The man reached into a box under the table and brought up half-a-dozen bundles like the one Teacup had given Thomas on their march to the camp.

"I need more than that. There's two of us," Teacup said, handing what was offered to Thomas for him to put in his bag.

"Can't hunt what'ch you need on da way?" The server smiled, showing black teeth.

"This time of year, on the way to the ruins? Use your head."

The smile faded. "Fine." The man grabbed six more bundles from another box, but hesitated before giving them to Teacup. "That's all you get. Waste'uh food—you ask me."

Teacup snatched the bundles. Reaching under her arm, she stuffed them into a side pocket on her backpack. "I need a bottle for this guy, too."

"Go fin' one." The server ladled a heaping spoonful of mystery food onto the plate of the next person in line.

"Come on." Teacup went to the generator.

There were tin cans around it, all partially full of the black gunk. She took one that was under a hose, catching oily drips, sticking the empty one she had in its place.

Thomas followed, glancing over his shoulder one last time at the food. "What is that?"

"Huh?" Teacup dipped her fingers into the can and rubbed the black goop on her face as she led him to the hallway.

"The stuff the guy was serving. What is it?"

"Mostly maggots. Some vegetables that still grow in the greenhouse. I think the chard and turnip are still growing."

Thomas grimaced. "Is that what I had yesterday?"

"What else would it be?" Teacup stopped at the bottom of the stairs to finish applying the war paint. When she was done she held out a filthy hand to Thomas. "Rag please?"

Thomas pulled one of the rags from his bag. He fought a gag as he handed it to her.

Teacup took it and wiped her hands with it. When they were as clean as she could get them, she wrapped the cloth over the top of the can and put it into her backpack. "Let's go."

It got noticeably colder as they climbed the stairs. Teacup shouldered open the door and a warrior on the other side flinched.

"Damn it, Cup. You're like a wild boar."

"Then my name should have been Boar." Teacup stopped next to him. "Like you've ever seen a boar anyway."

"What do you want?"

"I need your canteen for this guy. I have to take him to be presented."

The man huffed. "Fine. I want it back and you owe me three patrols." Leaning his spear against the wall, he fished out a canteen from a pack at his waist.

He handed the dented metal bottle to Thomas.

"Then I want your gloves, too," Teacup said.

"Not for him." The warrior watched as Thomas put the canteen in the satchel.

"No. Mine are being patched."

"Alright. But you get them fixed if you put a hole in them." He pulled off his gloves and flopped them into Teacup's open hand. "Good luck out there."

"Uh, huh." Teacup put on the gloves that were too big for her and led Thomas outside.

Snow from a Distant Sky

NINE
Fields of Snow

Once outside, Thomas could see the building and surrounding area more clearly in the dim light of day. Rooftops poked out from under the snow around them. He guessed the entrance they'd used had been roof access at some time in the past. What was visible looked like a school, matching the aesthetic in the cafeteria. A tower, most of it crumbled away, stood above the other peaks. A layer of ice covered one side of the tan brick.

The land sloped down to a field of ice with a narrow stream running through the middle of it. On the opposite side, the white bank rose up steeply.

Teacup headed away from the frozen river and up towards the surrounding forest. She nodded to the warriors on patrol as they passed. Before they made it into the tree line, she turned to Thomas.

"Better eat one of the rations now. I want to

make it to the edge of the wasteland before night-fall." She reached into a side pocket on her bag and pulled out a cloth bundle.

Thomas thought about the maggots and held off. The hunger pangs in his stomach gave up their fierce protest. He slipped and stumbled into one of the thin trees. It shook, dropping snow onto him from its branches above.

Shaking out his hood, he caught up to Teacup. "Isn't this all a wasteland?"

"I guess you could say that, but I'm talking about a place. Mostly empty and crumbling from the cold." Teacup used her spear like a walking stick, her steps leaving deep imprints in the crunching snow.

Thomas followed her footsteps, his heels carving shallow channels. "How far is it?"

"Day's walk if you can keep up with me. You should save your strength." She took a big bite of her ration.

Hearing the sound over the wind, Thomas winced. "How far to the capital after that?"

Teacup glanced behind her. "Save your strength means stop talking." She popped the rest of the maggot and chard chunk into her mouth.

They walked in silence through most of the day. Thomas lasted until the red orb, which he guessed was Mars, was high on the horizon before he broke down and ate one of his rations. The slimy sensation he'd ignored the day before consumed him as he chewed. Chomping until the chunk was paste, he swallowed and audibly gagged.

They walked through the forest for most of the morning, breaking out into open plains before he finished eating. Rolling hills stretched in front of them and Thomas wondered if the mounds were topographical or if they were made by things buried under the snow and ice.

He didn't ask, worried that he would annoy Teacup. She rarely looked back and when she did, she would scold him for falling behind.

You have a question? The words forced their way into his mind as the shadow spoke.

Thomas pulled his hood tighter and faced the ground, following Teacup's footprints. "How did you know?" he whispered.

I am getting more accustomed to you the longer you wear the robe.

"What does that mean?" Thomas furrowed his brow.

It is unimportant. You lack the requirements for true interface. Do you have questions? We did make a deal?

"I guess. I was wondering what the hills are made of."

Snow, obviously.

Thomas pressed his lips together. "I mean, what's under the snow."

My information is spotty, but there used to be a town in this area. The mounds may be the ruins of the buildings. Though, they could just be hills.

Thomas imagined the streets, cars and kids' bicycles deep below the drifts. "Why did the Healer say my necklace was useless if it's what brought me here."

That is not what brought you here. It is more like a key. It holds no value to people in need of food and fuel.

"Do you know about where I'm being taken?" Thomas slipped again. He landed in Teacup's wake and scrambled to his feet before she had a chance to check on him. He brushed his hands off on the robe and balled them up in the sleeves.

I lived in the city for a long time. Saw many strange things before the Earth was knocked from its orbit.

"What about now? What will they do to me at the capital?"

I have no idea. Though, the traveller who came before you may be able to help you, if she does not kill you for the gem and my cloak. The man I was bound to knew about the decree, to bring all travellers to the capital to be presented. It is a long-standing order. I doubt the tribe we just left would even know why. I have not been to the city in some time. I do not know what it will be like after so many years.

Still looking down at Teacup's trail, Thomas walked into her.

Reaching back, without looking, she grabbed his

collar to keep him from falling. "Quiet."

"What is it?" Thomas followed her gaze.

"I said be quiet," she said through clenched teeth.

I believe she is detecting a threat, the shadow said.

Thomas heard the sound of rhythmic crunching over the wind. He squinted, the reddish light shining off of the bright, undulating landscape.

In the distance he saw the shaggy beast. It lumbered over the crest of a large hill, its loping gait deceptively quick. It ran on four legs, its hindquarters sitting higher than its head. Long, tangled fur the colour of slush danced with each footfall. Thomas couldn't tell how big it was in the open field, but Teacup turned and ran.

She didn't call for him, hold his hand, or look back. As soon as she saw the beast, she left him and sprinted for a distant ridge.

Grabbing the hem of his robe, he ran after her. His shoes, made for pavement, lost traction. His heavy steps sunk into the deep snow. The monster closed in as Teacup pulled farther away.

Snow from a Distant Sky

TEN
Chasing Being Chased

Teacup reached the ridge and disappeared. Thomas ran after her, the blowing snow stinging his face and making it hard to see. Not wanting to know how close the monster was, and not wanting to trip again, he kept looking ahead.

When he reached the top of the ridge, he saw the remains of a town far below. Nestled next to a natural hill, the few unburied buildings were surrounded by mountains of snow. The cold and time had taken a toll. Crumbling facades exposed rotting interiors. Collapsed and hole-filled roofs let snow and ice into the structures.

The crumpled canopy of a gas station had fallen into a neighboring building, causing a chain reaction of destruction. Thomas spotted the small form of Teacup running towards the building on the far edge of the open crevice. The structure was partially consumed by the surrounding snow. A section of the roof was missing, but all four walls were intact.

Thomas scrambled after her, lost his footing, and slid the rest of the way down on his backside. The robe pulled up and snow filled his shorts. Ignoring the discomfort, he got to his feet as the slope leveled out, and charged for the building. He lost track of Teacup's footprints by the time he reached the wall.

"Teacup?" Running to the corner, he caught sight of the shambling creature barreling down the slope towards him.

The warrior yelled from the far end of the brick wall, next to the nearly sheer face of snow covering the structure. She waved to him before darting into the building. "Over here, hurry!"

Pawing at the wall as he ran, Thomas reached the door before the monster could catch him. He slammed a door behind him and leaned against it.

Teacup was farther inside the building, climbing a set of partially collapsed stairs. "What are you doing? Come on!"

Thomas left the door just as the beast slammed into it. The hinges gave and the wood split. Pieces of the door were thrown outward and Thomas had to duck to avoid a shard the size of his arm. It slammed into the back wall, leaving a hole.

The slobbering maw of the wild animal and one

of its massive paws reached through the open doorway at them. The creature rocked forward again and again, bashing against the wall, trying to force its way in. Cracks started to spread as the brick, mortar, and timber studs gave way.

Thomas crawled to the stairs and Teacup reached down from the landing to help pull him up. A step broke under him, but he clung to the railing with his free hand. With Teacup's help, he made it to the landing before the animal broke its way inside.

It let out a roar that Thomas felt in his bones. Teacup climbed up to the next floor and Thomas followed. The creature charged across the room and tried to follow up the narrow steps. The stairs crumbled up to the first landing, shaking the building. The beast jumped, digging its claws into the creaking wood. Before it could climb onto the landing, Teacup jumped from the top step and brought her spear down on its neck.

The rest of the stairs gave way and together with the huge beast, she dropped to the ground floor. Using the momentum, she drove the spear in deeper, rolled off of the struggling monster, and slashed her knife across its throat.

With a gurgling wail, it lashed out at her, but Teacup jumped back, out of its reach. She dodged another swing of its claws, and drove her knife into its side.

The animal stopped moving.

Thomas stood at the top of the open stairwell, staring down at the scene. He exhaled in a ragged breath and dropped to his knees.

How lucky you are to be accompanied by such a skilled warrior, the shadow said.

"Amazing." Thomas shivered. He was freezing. His shorts and underwear were soaked from sliding down the hill.

Teacup looked up at him, wiping her knife on the dense, shaggy fur of the slain animal. "Can you get down from there on your own?"

He nodded. "Yeah."

"Before you do, you should search that floor. We may as well spend the night here. We didn't make enough progress, but it'll be dark soon." Teacup went back to the beast at her feet. "Can't let this go to waste."

Thomas stayed on his knees looking over the warrior and her kill. He was out of breath. He thought about what he should keep an eye out for on the second floor, dawdling, until he saw her start to skin the creature.

Looking away, he got to his feet and groaned to himself to block out the sound.

The second floor seemed mostly intact to Thomas. The ceiling in the hallway was still there and while his footsteps creaked loudly and the floor felt unstable, it bore his weight. He went to the first door to opened it, but it was blocked. He tried to force his way into the room, but only managed to make the opening wide enough for him to see that the ceiling had collapsed.

Farther above, he could see the hole in the building's roof and the snow blowing inside. He gave up and continued his search. There were three more closed rooms and two larger open spaces. He figured the building had been an office and that it had been thoroughly picked through over the years. He managed to find a chipped bowl in a kitchenette that he stuck in his bag and some crumbling furniture in a break room that he dragged to the stairwell.

"There's not much up here, but I thought we could use this stuff to make a fire." Thomas stood around the wall out of sight of the ground floor.

"That should work. Come on down and get it started."

"Are you finished with, uh, butchering that thing?" Thomas swallowed, keeping down the slimy maggot mush he'd last eaten.

"I've got it skinned, but I'm still carving it. You can help me."

Clenching his eyes shut, Thomas grimaced. "I'd rather not. It's not something I'm used to."

Teacup sighed. "This will take a while. I want to bring as much with us as we can and bury the rest for when I make the trip home."

Thomas noticed she excluded him when she mentioned coming back. "Fine. I'll see if I can find anything else up here."

ELEVEN
When it Falls

Thomas hung out in the dilapidated break room while Teacup finished carving up the remains of the animal. His ears hurt from the cold, so he pulled the hood down as far as it could go. He stared at a pattern of mold that grew up the walls and around a cracked window and thought about what life would be like if he couldn't find a way home.

Imagining having to hunt and butcher his own food made him queasy. He wondered how useful he could be in the frozen, doomed world. He may know some things that they didn't, but he doubted his incomplete high school education would come in handy.

Reaching into his collar, he pulled out the yellow gem.

What occupies your thoughts? the shadow asked. It appeared in front of him in the same spot, just out of reach.

"I'm just thinking how useless I am. I don't know what being a traveller means." Twirling the gem between his fingers, he let the dim, reddish light shine through it. "Teacup seems to think it's a big deal."

It is not. The title came about as an attempt to categorize those unfortunate enough to leave their own worlds and end up here. Most worlds are not as bad off as this one.

"What about that traveller who built the capital?"

A remarkable person no matter what world she occupies.

Thomas let the gem go. It dropped to his chest and bounced before settling. "So, I'm just an unlucky guy with nothing to contribute?"

You are young, but as it stands, yes.

Leaning back, the rotting chair Thomas sat in shifted, threatening to break. "Got any guidance for me?"

Stay close to the warrior, but do not get attached.

"Why's that?"

The shadow took a while to answer. *For now, she is your best chance at survival.*

The room grew dark. Thomas looked away from the shadow, then rubbed his eyes.

If you value your life over others, there may come a time where you must sacrifice her to save yourself. I do not know what fate awaits you in the capital. She may be taking you to your death.

Thomas could feel his mouth dry out. The thought of dying or having to make a choice about sacrificing himself or betraying someone seemed so foreign. He thought about the TV shows he'd binged and the video games he'd played. Then he thought of the beast that had chased him and how Teacup left him behind.

The sound of the wavering wind changed to a roar that would have deafened the cry of the monster. Snow assaulted the window and over the wind, he heard the sound of impact, like rocks tumbling out of the back of a dump truck.

The walls and floors swayed, buffeted by the growing squall, and the room went black as the window was blotted out.

"Thomas, get down here!" The noise of the storm muted Teacup's shout.

Thomas felt his way down the hallway to the open stairwell. He saw the flickering light of a fire and stopped next to the pile of broken furniture he'd left on the landing.

Teacup looked up at him from the ground floor. She had taken off her pelt, but was still coated in the used oil. "Come on. The storm looks bad."

"Okay. Move back." Thomas shoved the broken furniture over the edge then lowered himself down. A small fire crackled at the buried end of the building. In the light, he saw the lake of blood where Teacup had butchered the animal and the drag marks that led to the bloody remains by the smashed open doorway. Snow and sleet piled up at the entrance and the vicious wind pushed it across the floor.

"Good thing we have food. We'll bury what's left before we leave."

"What's left?" Thomas pulled his gaze away from the gore. "How long do storms usually last?"

Teacup shrugged and headed to the fire. "Days. Longer. We're in a good place, though. Even if the building collapses, a fair bit is already buried, so this part should hold up. We have food, and we should be able to keep the fire going for a while." She sat against a nearby wall. "It's lucky the shambler chased us in here."

"And that you were able to kill it." Thomas sat on the opposite side of the fire, his back to the room.

Teacup shrugged. "I've dealt with them before. I'd much rather fight a shambler than be stuck outside when the snow falls." Reaching up, she vigorously scratched her head with both hands, leaving her hair standing on end. "Our biggest problem now is having a way out."

Thomas looked over his shoulder at the doorway, made wider by the monster. Rather than the icy pellets that were picked up in the constant breeze, the falling snow was made up of fat flakes that quickly collected in piles and clung to everything.

"We have a while before we have to start digging. This area is fairly protected, being sunk in like this." Teacup tossed a chair leg onto the fire. "We'd better get some sleep while we can. If it's a bad one, we'll be digging until it's over. I'll take first watch."

"Okay." Hesitantly, Thomas shimmied to the wall and got into the same position he had been the night before in Teacup's small room. Pulling his hood low, he crossed his arms. He doubted that he would sleep. He was still wired from being chased and he hadn't felt safe since appearing in the frozen world. But, his head dropped. After a few startled jerks, he dozed off.

Snow from a Distant Sky

TWELVE
Dig

Thomas woke shivering. He could feel the moisture from his breath frozen to his face. Lifting his head, he groaned through a stretch. The fire burned low, the cinders sparkling in the cold.

Teacup wasn't there. Her spear and bag were propped against the wall. Bracing himself, Thomas rolled onto his side and stood. The cold had seeped into his bones and his joints ached. Most of the room was in shadow. The dwindling fire was the only source of light. Scanning the room, he noticed the mound of snow near the doorway was much larger than it had been when he went to sleep.

Rubbing his hands together, he meandered towards the pile. When he was close, he heard the sound of muted digging. Slowly, he stuck his head into the doorway.

"Teacup?"

On the other side of the opening, a tunnel extended out half-a-metre before angling up sharply. Thomas ducked farther into the passage. Reaching the incline, he shimmied onto his side and looked up.

"Teacup?" He bit on the name, nervous saying it out loud.

A heap of snow the size of a small bag of flour dropped into his face.

"Don't call me that," Teacup said, her voice dull in the tunnel.

Thomas scrambled back into the building, wiping the snow from his eyes and blowing it out of his nose.

A moment later, Teacup landed at the bottom of the incline. "Did I get you?" The tar was streaked down her face, her exposed skin was red. Her hair was plastered to her head and steam radiated from her.

Nodding, Thomas pulled back his hood and turned it inside out.

"Sorry. It came down harder last night and I figured I should get started before we got trapped in here." Teacup took off her borrowed gloves and tucked them into her waistband. She went to the pile of broken furniture, picked up a chair with a missing leg, and smashed it against the wall. Collecting the pieces, she brought them to the fire. "Time for some food, then I'll get back to it."

Blowing on the embers, she got the scrap-wood to light. "Bring something else." She waved Thomas over. "The chair's going up quickly."

Thomas hurried to the pile and dragged half a broken table from it. He wrenched off a leg and brought it to her.

Teacup took it, snapped it in half over her knee, and tossed both pieces into the roaring fire. "How'd you sleep?"

Grabbing his sore neck, Thomas shrugged. "Why didn't you wake me?"

"You seemed pretty tired. The snow buried us, so I wasn't worried about anyone getting the drop on us."

"I can go dig for a bit." Thomas turned to walk away, but Teacup grabbed the hem of his robe.

"You should eat first."

Thinking of the rations, Thomas felt for the bag over his shoulder. It had shifted in his sleep, but he was still wearing it. "I'm okay."

"You're going to burn out if you don't take care of yourself." Teacup let him go. "I don't know many people who would turn down fresh meat." Scooting over to her bag, she pulled out a bundle that was red with blood. Unwrapping it, she stabbed the meat with her knife.

She held it to the fire, her forearm resting on her

knee. "Go on, unless you changed your mind."

The warmth of the growing blaze and the smell of the charring meat held Thomas in place. His mouth watered and his stomach gurgled painfully. He looked away, his face warm.

Something landed at his feet. He looked and saw another red bundle. Slowly, he got to his haunches and picked up the package. "Thank you."

"You know how to cook it to burn out the toxins?"

He shook his head.

"Have a seat and I'll show you."

Thomas dropped to his butt and crossed his legs. "I'll take the next digging shift, though."

Teacup smiled like an adult pretending to let a child win. "Get your knife."

The meat was greasy and the faint smell of urine clung to his fingers. He'd eaten moose when his parents had taken him on vacation up north the year before, and the shambler tasted similarly gamey. Not unpleasant, but unusual.

As soon as he finished eating, Thomas slapped his knees and went to the tunnel to take his shift digging. The meat felt heavy in his stomach as he crawled up the incline and reached the end of the tunnel.

Taking out his worn and grease-covered knife, he gouged out wedges of the packed snow, letting it drop down below him. Using his newly scavenged bowl, he scooped the sides. When his hands burned from the cold and his cheeks were stiff, he wormed his way down, pushing the accumulated snow back into the building.

"Just need a minute to warm up and I'll get back to it," he said, approaching the fire. Across the crackling flames, he saw Teacup on her side, the backpack like a pillow under her head. He split the broken table top into pieces and added them to the fire. He stood as close to it as he could to warm up.

When he could feel his fingers, he went back to digging.

He wasn't sure how long he'd been at it, but after a few cycles of digging and warming himself at the fire, he managed to break through to the surface. It was dark and the wind buffeted him with chilled wafts that penetrated the robe. The stars gleamed overhead, but like with the extra suns in the day, something about the night felt off.

It had stopped snowing, but the wind carried the sharp speckles of ice with it and pressed the hood against his face. Thomas did his best to orient himself in the altered landscape. The slope up to the fields of rolling hills was in front of him, but was much less steep after the blizzard. To his left, he saw the collapsed gas station below him. The snow had shrunk the exposed section of the town, burying the building where he and Teacup had run to when the beast chased them. He took a few steps towards the dark remains of the town, his feet creaking in the snow.

He looked up at the stars. In his own world, the best he could hope for on a clear night would be to find the big dipper.

Wondering about the sky? The shadow appeared, blotting out a section of stars.

Thomas managed to keep himself from flinching. "Yes."

The moon is gone. Spun off on its own doomed trajectory.

Staring up, his neck craned, Thomas felt unsteady on his feet. He didn't think the news had shocked him. Not any more than the idea that he was in a totally different world. He took an unsteady step back as another gust pushed against him.

She is coming, the shadow said. *And by the sound of her crawling, I suspect she is displeased.* It vanished back into the robe.

Thomas traced his footsteps back to the hole. He watched Teacup climb to the surface, spear preceding her.

She zeroed in on him and closed the distance with a purposeful gait. "What do you think you're doing?" She whispered, but the words were harsh.

"I made it to the top." He frowned at her.

"It's dangerous out here. There could be another shambler. What if a gang was looking for stragglers after the storm? You should've woke me up."

Thomas took a deep breath that chilled his lungs, but his protest caught in his throat. "I was trying to be useful."

The anger drained out of Teacup. "It's going to be night for a while. We should go sit by the fire as long as we can. The next leg of the trip is risky." She turned and headed for the hole.

"What should I call you?" Thomas asked.

"Huh?" Teacup stopped and looked back at him.

"You got mad at me when I called you… Before, when I woke up."

Teacup stared ahead of her. "I don't care."

"That's not true."

"I don't like my name. My father called me that and everyone else picked up on it. Now, I only let superiors get away with it." She crossed her arms.

Thomas walked past her towards the hole. "Fine, but it'll be weird if I don't have anything to call you."

Teacup caught up. "You can call me Cup, I guess. Only because I won't see you after this." She stopped at the hole and stuck the butt end of her spear in the snow. "After you."

Thomas crawled in backwards and Teacup followed, blocking up the entrance behind her.

Snow from a Distant Sky

THIRTEEN
Sunset

In the morning, Teacup crawled into the tunnel ahead of Thomas. Using her spear, she cleared the exit and waited. Thomas shivered behind her. Icy wind found its way into the hole and howled its way past them.

Thomas shifted his satchel. It was weighed down with meat from the creature that had chased them and the strap pulled on his neck.

"Why aren't we moving?" he whispered.

Teacup looked past her knees at him. "Because I'm not a reckless kid eager to be ambushed." She poked her head over the lip of the hole and shimmied in a complete circle.

"See anything?"

She shushed him and held her spear high in the air. "Be ready to run. We're going to head south. Don't stop until we reach the trees."

Without waiting for Thomas to reply, Teacup climbed to the surface and disappeared.

Scrambling after her, Thomas held his heavy satchel in one arm and followed the best he could.

The two suns and Mars were behind the incline to their left, but the reddish glow painted the white ground. The frigid temperatures of the opaque night hung on against the weak light.

Thomas could feel the cold burning his lungs as he huffed, slipping and scrabbling after Teacup. He glanced at the high ground surrounding them, expecting to see another huge shaggy silhouette or the shapes of the wild people she had warned him about.

The path in front of them rose up, but not as sharply as the hills on either side. Teacup was getting farther ahead, her pace steady. Thomas' speed waned.

Gritting his teeth, Thomas slowed his mad sprint. He paid attention to his footfalls, trading speed for stability. He extended his steps and steadied his breathing. Teacup was too far ahead for him to catch, but he managed to slow the growing gap between them.

He stopped looking around him and focused on the path she'd carved into the snow. The clear tracks felt normal to him. He realized that if she left him that he would have a limited amount of time to find her before the wind and snow covered any trace of her. He wouldn't be able to find his way back to her tribe, or even to the buried building.

Eventually, the effort of running and breathing was enough to consume all his thoughts. His vision narrowed to the tracks and a sliver of the horizon in his periphery. Trees came into view. Slender, like all the ones he'd seen, but less densely packed together.

As he got closer, he saw a figure wearing a dirty pelt on her shoulders, the open jaws of the animal resting on her head. He hoped it was Teacup and that the strange way of wearing the pelt was something specific to her tribe.

He collapsed, sliding to a stop at her feet. Head swimming, he rolled onto his side and spat gobs of saliva. He wiped his mouth with his sleeve and closed his eyes.

Teacup said something, but the words were fuzzy.

She said you should stand. You will catch your breath faster, the shadow said in his head.

Thomas took his time getting to his feet. Sparkles that reminded him of the translucent portal danced across his vision. Teacup put an arm around him and helped him walk farther into the forest. By the time the open field was out of sight, he could walk on his own.

"Sorry. I didn't think I was that out of shape."

He leaned against a tree.

Teacup jammed her spear into the snow. "The cold is harsh if you're not used to it." She pulled the bottle out of her pack and drank. "We'll have to adjust our pace, which means we have a long day of walking ahead of us."

Crouching, she stuffed snow into the bottle until it was full, shook it a few times, and put it back into her backpack. "This snow is fresh from the blizzard. You should fill up too."

She waited for him to fill his canteen, then led him deeper into the forest. "Try to keep up, and tell me if you can't."

They walked until the suns and Mars were setting, stopping once to pee. They ate maggot rations on the move. Thomas was so tired and hungry, he didn't mind the taste or texture. The thought of what was in the slimy nuggets still turned his stomach, but they kept him going at Teacup's steady march.

She stopped at a rocky outcrop where a few of the spindly trees had fallen, knocking into others like improbable dominos. "We should rest here and cook something more substantial while we can. It's going to be harder going in the dark."

Thomas sat on one of the logs. It sank deeper into the snow, but he was too tired to care. His feet were completely numb up to his ankles, but he was sure he had blisters from walking in wet socks.

"I don't want to say that was short, but the days go by really quickly." He took sips from his canteen. The water was half-frozen into slush and hurt his throat.

"Shorter every year." Teacup took out her knife and hacked at the fallen trees, cutting off branches. When she had an armful, she piled them next to the outcropping and lit a fire.

Thomas left the thin log and sat as close to the fire as he could. "How long do we have?"

"We can maybe spare an hour." Teacup left the fire to collect more wood.

"Ugh, good." Thomas took two of the skinny branches from the pile before they could catch. He skewered shambler steaks onto one end and stuck the other into the snow so the meat would roast over the fire. When he was sure the skewers were stable, he took off his shoes and socks.

His feet were red and raw and he could see several blisters on both. He lay the satchel next to the fire and rested his feet on it, holding them to the flames. Laying his socks on his running shoes, he put them close as well.

Teacup came back with larger logs. She stoked the fire and added the wood on top. Sitting next to Thomas, she spun the skewers. "Your shoes are so impractical."

"For the snow." Thomas rubbed his feet, forcing

the blood to circulate. "If I knew I was coming here, I'd have dressed for it. And packed some camping gear."

"So you didn't come here on purpose?"

Leaning back, Thomas wiggled his toes. "No." He grimaced through a cramp.

"Do you mind telling me how it happened?" Teacup focused on cooking the meat.

"I can tell you what I know." Thomas fished out the necklace. "My uncle was a traveller—world traveller. Not to different worlds. I don't think." He stared at the gem as it caught the firelight.

"He said he got this for me somewhere in India. He loved going there. Said it never got the credit for what it gave to the world. Science, math, engineering. He said there were a lot of secrets still to uncover there."

"That rock." Teacup nodded to the gem. "Has something to do with it?"

Thomas took off the necklace and handed it to her. "He gave it to me for my birthday."

"Birthday? The day you were born?"

"Yeah, but where I come from, you celebrate that day every year. My birthday was a few weeks ago and he came home to give me that. After my parents went to bed, he brought me to the attic. He had all kinds of things stored up there."

Teacup looked up from the gem. "What's an

attic?"

"A space under the roof of a house."

"Okay."

Thomas grunted and bent his knees so the sides of his feet were closer to the fire. "Anyway. He told me the gem had something to do with opening doors and that I should keep it safe." Thomas smiled. "He always said stuff like that. He'd give me a trinket and make me think it was special. I guess I liked to believe it because I started wearing it. I'd keep it under my shirt. I didn't want people to make fun of me at school, but I liked having it.

"One day, I saw a light inside the gem. It got brighter the closer I got to the basketball court. Then, I was here."

Teacup thrust the slices of meat deeper into the flames. "I didn't understand a lot of that." She held the necklace back to him.

"I could explain the stuff about school and basketball." He took it and put it back around his neck.

She shook her head. "No." Standing, she held one of the skewers to him. "I should make sure no one is around to see the smoke. Especially with you like that."

Thomas took the skewer and she left, eating as she went.

Snow from a Distant Sky

FOURTEEN
Tight Fit

Thomas had no way to tell time and the suns and Mars, which never rose higher than the bottom quarter of the sky, moved too fast for him to guess. In the growing dark of nightfall, he couldn't tell how long Teacup had been patrolling the area. When she came back, she kicked snow on the fire without a word and stared at him until he got his socks and shoes back on.

His socks had dried, but they were stiff from dirt and sweat. The sole on one shoe had slightly melted, too. The blisters on his feet hurt when he hurried after Teacup, but he was glad that he could feel his toes again.

They walked in silence, Teacup going just fast enough for Thomas to have to work to keep up, but not so fast that she left him behind. He trusted her to know where they were going and to be able to

spot pitfalls in their path since he couldn't see anything in the moonless dark.

They reached the edge of the woods and headed
out into the open. The speckled swath of the Milky
Way was the brightest source of light. Thomas
scanned it back and forth, not looking for anything
specific, but taking in the faint illumination.

With his head inclined, ice blew into his hood
and trickled down into the cloak. He couldn't stop
shivering as the temperature continued to drop, but
the thin fabric was enough to keep him going.

When he finally looked down, he saw a huge
shadow on the horizon. It would have been invisible,
but it was so large that it touched the star-strewn sky,
blotting out vertical stripes of it.

He jogged to catch up with Teacup who had put
some distance between them as he stargazed.

"What's that?" Thomas pointed at the silhouette.

Teacup huffed and Thomas could feel the moisture from her breath as the wind blew it at him. "The
ruins," she said.

Thomas hesitated, his steps catching in the snow.
"Ruins of what?"

"The old settlement."

"That looks pretty big to be a settlement. How
far away is it?"

Teacup reached into the pelt and scratched her
scalp. "It's very big. If we can get to the next thicket

and find a cave to sleep in for the rest of the night, we should be able to get to the outskirts by the morning."

"What if we don't get to the thicket tonight?"

"I'll get there. If you can't keep up, you'll freeze."

Thomas fell in behind her. He swore he could feel the cold more than he had before she pointed it out. He adjusted the satchel and crossed his arms, tucking his hands into the sleeves.

They continued at the same pace, Teacup's steps as consistent as a robot, until they reached the next tree line. Once in the cover of the thin trunks, she slowed and waved him forward.

Leaning close, she whispered in his ear. "Keep an eye open for tracks. We're close enough to the ruins that there could be people here. If you see anyone other than me, defend yourself. They'll kill you if you're lucky."

She walked slowly onward, her steps high and measured. Thomas gripped the strap of his bag and considered taking out the old knife she'd given him.

They picked their way forward, Teacup stopping and starting, like a predator on the hunt, and Thomas wide-eyed, looking for anything in the pitch-black thicket.

They reached a ridge of rock that jutted out of the snow like the bony scales of a stegosaurus.

Teacup got low and shuffled under a scale of

rock and down into a shallow crevice. A moment later, she crawled out again.

"This will work. Get in and go as far back as you can. It's going to be a tight fit."

Thomas did what she said. He got down on his hands and knees and shimmied into the gap. After a few moments, Teacup followed, pushing him in deeper until he was worried that he would get stuck.

"I can't go any farther." He pulled at the strap of the satchel, but the bulk of the bag was wedged behind him.

"You're not that big." She gave him a shove and he slid in more, his arms getting pinned at his side. She lay on top of him, her shoulder on his chest, and positioned the pelt over her like a blanket.

Thomas cleared his throat. "Um."

"What?"

He shut his eyes tightly. "I'm not saying that I'm claustrophobic, but I'm not awesome when I can't move my arms."

"It's this, freeze, or get ambushed." She shifted.

Her weight on top of him was reassuring, even though he desperately wanted out. Swallowing, he took long breaths in through his nose and out his mouth. He could smell the oil on her. It was intense at first, but he got used to it as he breathed. He thought of her warmth next to him, trying to block out the panic at the periphery. Then, he panicked for a different reason. It was the first time he'd been so close to a girl that he wasn't related to since he was a child.

Biting his lip, he thought of the shambling beast chasing them, of the sour maggot chunks he'd eaten, the numbing cold, and the blisters on his feet.

Then he heard her snoring and the worry subsided. It wasn't loud, but with her so close, her face high up on his chest, he could feel the rumbling.

That was a close one, the shadow said.

Thomas turned his head away so he spoke into the rock. "Could you tell?"

Not physically, but it was obvious. Do you have any questions for me?

"The ruins." Thomas tried to keep his chest from moving too much as he whispered. "Is it a city?"

Long ago. A great city that spanned the coast.

"And it's dangerous?"

Very. The capital lies within, an island of order in the sea of chaos and ruin.

"And the people Teacup mentioned?"

Cannibals. Raiders. De-evolved savages, even more so than this one whose proximity causes you excitement.

Thomas could feel his face flush. "How long is a day?"

Twenty-four hours.

"I mean how much sunlight is there in a day?"

I assume you mean how long is there light. In the autumn months, as it is now, this region receives approximately seven hours of daylight. Less and less each day. In fact, there may never be more sun in a day ever again.

His eyes still closed, Thomas yawned. "Is there anything I can do to help? To stop it?"

Help is relative but what is happening to this planet cannot be stopped by any human civilization that I have heard of.

"You know about other worlds? Other than mine?"

Only through hearsay. You should sleep while you can. You have a long, dangerous walk again tomorrow.

Despite his discomfort, fatigue overwhelmed Thomas.

FIFTEEN
True
Substance

Teacup pulled Thomas from the crevice while it was still dark out. It had been a warmer night once their body heat cut the chill in the rocks, but he was stiff and sore from being squeezed into the tight space with her on top of him.

They started walking right away, munching on rations. Thomas' eyes hurt, like they were too dry. His eyelids were heavy and he dragged his feet until his body accepted that he was awake for the day.

The over-glow of sunrise illuminated the horizon. The red light hitting the thin trees created long shadows in the sparse woods. Thomas watched the foreign sun crested the snowy landscape, followed by the one he'd known, and the much larger Mars. With the suns low, he could make out more surface features of the red planet. The massive volcano and the deep canyons were soon washed out by the blooming light and he was left unsure if he'd even seen them at all.

In the distance in front of them, Thomas could see the hazy outline of the city Teacup called the ruins. Blowing snow made the view hazy, like a television station that wouldn't come in clearly.

If they were still a day's walk to the outskirts like Teacup had told him, the buildings he could see were huge. The scene was predominantly vertical, but there were horizontal aberrations, as if the tops of some of the skyscrapers had fallen and were wedged between the buildings. He would have sworn that some of the buildings were being held up by their neighbours.

He didn't notice the forest around them was thinning until the number of cut down stumps out-numbered tall, thin trees.

The wind picked up with less to block it and there were more dune-like drifts—some taller than Thomas.

Teacup stopped. "I need a minute." She handed him the spear.

The freezing metal felt almost hot in Thomas' bare hand. He used the long sleeves of the robe as a buffer. "What for?"

"I gotta go." Teacup headed for the nearest tall dune. "Keep an eye out."

Catching her drift, Thomas nodded stiffly and

scanned the forest in the opposite direction of the dune.

He wasn't sure how far she'd gone, but all he could hear was the sound of the wind. The suns were already nearing the peak of their trajectory. Thomas held his hand up to them, as if he could measure how much more sunlight they would have that day.

There was a crunch behind him as someone stepped in a patch of hard snow. He turned, expecting Teacup, and held the spear out, ready to give it back.

Instead, the shaft of the spear intercepted the swing of a club.

The spear was knocked from his hand and Thomas stared at a skinny man missing most of his nose.

He had filthy rags wrapped around him in thick layers and the exposed part of his face was red with black patches of frostbite.

Thomas jumped back as the man lifted the club over his head. The hand gripping the rough handle was missing fingers but the swing was hard and fast. Thomas could feel the breeze as it sailed past his face.

Someone grabbed Thomas from behind, the thin arms surprisingly strong. Rocking forward, Thomas tried to break the hold and slipped, taking the assailant to the ground with him. He wriggled and fought but couldn't escape.

The satchel had flopped on top of him and though his arms were held, he could reach the side pocket where he'd stashed the old knife.

Still writhing, he slipped his fingers into the pocket and managed to grip the knife between them. The thin blade slipped out easily, but the person holding him heaved, as if trying to drag Thomas to his feet, and the knife dropped to the snow.

Thomas caught sight of the man with the club swing down at him. Furiously kicking out, Thomas managed to push himself and the person holding him out of the way.

He ended up on top, the arms still around him like a vice. Rocking forward, he brought his head back as hard as he could and the grip lessened enough for him to pull an arm free.

Grabbing the knife, he stabbed blindly behind him and the arms let go. Thomas scrambled to his feet. Slipping, he swiped at the man with the club, keeping him back.

The person on the ground held their leg, blood seeping into their filthy rag clothing.

Thomas turned and ran for the dune. "Cup!"

Before he could reach the base of the hill, he felt the club come down on his head. He fell face first into the snow, dazed.

Feeling as if he were under water, he rolled onto his side, still holding the knife.

The tattered shape of the rag-covered man wrenched the blade free and stuck it into a belt. More thin, gangly people in tattered clothing crawled out from the snow or behind dunes. Some came to help the frostbitten man haul Thomas to his feet, but a few went to the person Thomas had stabbed.

Thomas was bound, his hands behind his back like when Teacup had first caught him. He thought of her and hoped she was okay. His head hurt and his focus was muddled. The image of her in his mind was blended with a girl from his school who used to tease him.

Several hands grabbed onto him and pulled him forward. Thomas walked on unsteady legs, his feet dragging in the deep snow.

He wasn't sure how long he was urged forward, but his head gradually cleared. The pain from being struck by the club stayed with him, though. It radiated out from the point of impact at the back of his skull.

He counted eight individuals all dressed in tattered, layers of clothes, but they moved around each other constantly, disappearing behind mounds of snow or rock, slipping behind him and appearing on the other side.

Eventually, they reached the first ruined buildings at the edge of the city. They didn't seem remarkable to Thomas. The street looked like something from his world, but old and forgotten. It was uncomfortable to see, like the aftermath of a natural disaster, or a warzone, but coated in ice and snow.

The huge buildings he'd seen on the horizon were still indistinct shapes in the distance, mostly obstructed by the city around him. There were more rag-people in the broken windows and empty doorways. It was like they were coming out to greet the returning heroes, or to see the oddity they brought back with them.

Thomas couldn't tell if the thin, hunched people were men or women, but he could see the ravages of the frozen world in their exposed faces and amputations.

The wind howled through the open street, piling the snow against the buildings. The light posts seemed short. Thomas guessed that with all the compacted layers of snow under their feet, the lamps were only five metres above him.

He imagined there were cars, mailboxes, benches, and garbage bins buried below him. It made the street feel empty.

The people dragged him around a corner and into an alley. There was an angled hole dug into the snow that led down to a set of double doors at the back of a building. They took him inside and dropped him at the feet of another identically clothed figure.

"Good. You got the traveller, just as the wizard predicted." The words came out as rasps. Thomas thought it must hurt the person to talk.

The figure reached out a wrapped hand to him. The pinky finger was missing and Thomas thought part of the ring finger too. He recoiled, but the people who had brought him there held him in place.

The hand extended into his robe and took the necklace from around his neck.

Holding it up to a torch, the figure clutched the chain tightly, as if afraid to lose it. "This is it. Get the wizard."

Snow from a Distant Sky

SIXTEEN
A Wizard on Strings

Thomas expected another robe-clad wizard to walk into the firelight and shoot lightning. Instead, three rag-people wheeled a squeaking table to the top of a few steps.

They turned a crank and the back of the table slowly rose. Chains rattled and gears clicked as the tall, gangly thing came into view. The wizard was tied to the table with a dozen scraps of filthy cloth. It didn't look human in the dim light. It had the vague shape of a person with arms and legs, but metal and plastic protrusions stuck out of the body, as if it had been impaled a hundred times.

It looked dead, but when the table was nearly vertical, its masked head lifted off its chest. Cables, like hair, rattled as they cascaded across its shoulders.

"The wizard of the plains must have fallen if this one wears its robes."

If the rag person holding the gem talked with a rasp, the wizard strapped to the table screeched. Thomas thought it sounded like a kid's toy with a broken speaker. Robotic, fuzzy, and eerie.

The leader of the rag-people waved a thin arm and the others left. "Do your job and I may grant you the robe."

The wizard didn't move, like it was processing what the leader said. After enough time for Thomas to start fidgeting, it spoke. "I did as I was asked. I found you a traveller and you already hold the key. Free me."

"You live because I believe you can still be useful," the leader croaked. He, or she, Thomas had no idea, doubled over in a coughing fit, staining the face rags red. "You can't even move. What would freedom be to you?"

"Give me the robe and see."

Thomas stayed on his knees. He struggled to see the wizard in the dancing light. The room beyond the flames was a mystery. He could tell the building was in bad shape and filled with clutter. The floor had slick patches that, in the orange illumination, could have been from oil or blood.

The pain in his head was steady and his heart raced, but he could think more clearly. The satchel he'd borrowed from Teacup was gone, but the meat and rations didn't seem important in the moment.

He spared a thought for the warrior, though. At first hoping that she was okay, then deluding himself with a fantasy of her coming to his rescue.

The gem would likely work for anyone, not just him. But he didn't know if they knew.

I would prefer to not fall into the hands of that one. Not that he is able to move his hands anymore, the shadow said in Thomas' head.

The intrusive thoughts punctuated his headache. He whispered as quietly as he could. "Why not?"

He was a monster long before this world came to pass.

The wizard may have looked his way, Thomas couldn't tell. The leader in rags brought the gem to the vertical table.

"How do I use it?"

"It is not a thing to be wielded." The voice of the wizard cut out and was replaced with a static-shriek.

The leader smacked the wizard hard in the head. "Pay attention."

The sound died like the final moments of a storm siren. Slowly, the wizard faced Thomas. "The gem is like a ticket. It allows the wielder to pass through a portal."

"How do I know you aren't lying?"

"You don't."

The leader pulled down the rag covering its mouth and spat. The dark gob hit the floor with a splat. "The boy—the traveller. What role does he play?"

"None."

"So anyone could use the key?"

This is looking bad for you.

"Should I run?" Thomas whispered.

Do you think you can get past the others outside?

Thomas gritted his teeth. His wrists hurt from being tied up, but he could stand and try to sneak out. The leader wasn't looking at him and he wasn't sure if the wizard could even see.

The wizard sputtered out more noise that broke into words. "That is what I know."

Do not forget your goal. The shadow said. *You will not be able to get home without the gem.*

Sighing, Thomas let his shoulders drop. "Is the wizard right? About the gem?"

As far as I am aware, yes. He should not know any more about it than I do.

"What do you know about it?"

It was part of an experiment gone wrong.

Thomas scratched his nose against his shoulder. "Did it have anything to do with what happened? The earth becoming a rogue planet?"

That is an unfortunate coincidence.

The leader turned. It moved its shoulders, but kept its head trained on Thomas, like a bird of prey. "What are you saying over there? Who are you talking to?"

Thomas looked away. "I'm not. I'm just scared."

Snapping its wrapped head towards the wizard, the leader grabbed the table. "Who is the traveller speaking to?"

The wizard didn't answer and the leader hit him repeatedly.

"Answer me! I'll bury you again! Leave you to rot in the snow!" The leader hacked and coughed, but kept hitting the bound wizard.

"He is probably speaking with the entity that inhabits the robe," the wizard said passively while his head rocked from the impacts.

The leader stopped the attack. "And what is this entity?"

"Something from when the city was alive."

"Does it have knowledge? Can it tell me what you can't?" Letting go of the table, the leader crouched and lumbered towards Thomas.

"It has fragmented information from the past. It is useless to you without me. Give me the robe and I will help you escape this world."

Still closing on Thomas, the leader hissed over its shoulder. "You do not give me orders. I will see what this one knows for myself."

With a grunt, Thomas got his feet under him and retreated from the tattered leader. He backed to the door, keeping his eyes on the stalking figure.

Stumbling over something, he looked down and the leader pounced.

Though thin, the person was as savage and unexpectedly strong like the others. At first, it tried to get hold of the robe, but with fingers missing and its hands in bandages, it didn't seem to be able to grip the fabric.

Thomas squirmed. He tried to scrabble back, roll onto his side, kick the thing off of him, but the leader held on.

Giving up on the robe, the leader screeched and brought its fists down on Thomas indiscriminately. The blows weren't particularly strong, but they kept falling, hitting him in the face, neck, and chest.

You must escape. Fight back.

The wizard screamed, his words breaking up like a skipping CD. "Bring me the robe. Kill him if you must."

Thomas tucked in his chin, his eyes tightly shut. He thrashed and his foot caught something, jolting him back enough to throw the leader off balance. Yelling, he bucked the thin figure off of him and tucked in his knees, getting his hands in front of him.

He swung his fists striking the leader before it could pounce again.

Turning, he ran for the door, the wizard and leader screaming in dissonance.

The gem. The shadow reminded him.

Thomas dashed to the upright table. The wizard turned his head in jerky motions to follow the action. Ignoring the creepy thing, Thomas scanned the floor for the chain.

"Looking for this?" The leader held the gem over its head. "I will escape this doomed world and you won't stop me!"

Thomas lunged, reaching for the gem with his bound hands. The leader snarled and grabbed for the robe. Thomas considered slipping out of the robe in the hopes of distracting the leader and getting the gem. It was cold outside, but he needed the gem to get home more than he needed the shadow.

There was a chance he could lose both. Before he could make up his mind, the doors burst open.

Snow from a Distant Sky

114

SEVENTEEN
Rescue Mission

The faint light of the coming dusk shone down the tunnel and in through the wide-open doorway. Teacup, as if bringing the reddish glow with her, quickly scanned the room and locked in on Thomas struggling with the leader of the rag-people.

She barreled into them, sending the leader to the floor and holding Thomas up by his arm. "What are you doing? We have to go!"

"The gem." Thomas dove at the prone, rag-wrapped leader and continued the struggle.

"It's a rock." Teacup grabbed him by the scruff. "It's not even that pretty."

Thomas ignored her and the robe digging into his neck. "It's my way home," he said, choking out the words.

The leader growled like a starving animal. "It is my salvation!"

"Fine." Teacup let go of Thomas and stepped on the thin, bandaged arm of the leader. Bending down with the same exasperation as a mother taking something from an unruly child, she snatched the necklace. "If you want it back, you have to come with me."

The fight seemed to leave the leader.

Thomas disengaged and stood. "Fine with me."

Teacup went back through the doorway.

"Wait. You are taking away the only chance to save my people. We will suffer and die without that key." The leader reached for him even though Thomas was too far away.

Thomas paused at the door.

"Come on!" Teacup yelled from the top of the tunnel.

"I'm sorry." Thomas kept his head down as he followed Teacup.

She ran to the end of the alley and checked around the corner. "I'm sure a bunch of them saw me and are on their way."

Thomas caught up and leaned against the wall.

"You okay?" she asked.

He nodded. "My head hurts, but I'm fine. I'm glad you're alright." Huffing, he kicked the wall with his heel. "I screwed up. I'm sorry."

"I should have seen the ambush."

There was the sound of crunching snow around

the corner. "Now's not the time," Teacup said, facing the direction of the noise. "Do you know what happened to my spear?"

"No."

She shook her head, took out her knife, and cut the rags around his wrists. "Too bad. Get your knife ready in case."

"Someone took it." Thomas balled up the sleeve of the robe in his hand. "In the struggle." With his hands free, he realized that he wouldn't have been able to take the robe off in the scuffle with the leader when he was bound, and felt his cheeks flush.

Teacup glanced back at him. "That was my first knife." She sighed. "Get ready to run."

A bandaged figure dropped behind Thomas. It was thin and mutilated like the others. It could have even been the one who first attacked him. Thomas looked up to see where it came from and saw a rusted balcony overhead.

The person lunged, something in its hand reflecting the waning light.

Thomas jumped back, bumping into Teacup. They stumbled out into the snow-packed street where more of the cloth-covered people were waiting.

Teacup stabbed the first one to get close. The person dropped, clutching a belly wound.

The rest of them swarmed, but some stopped

at the one who was injured. Thomas watched them pull the coverings from their faces, exposing their black and scarred mouths. He turned away as soon as he saw them bite down on their injured companion.

The footfalls from the ones who continued to chase them sounded like an avalanche barreling down on them. Catching up with Teacup, he managed to keep pace.

"Don't slow down," she said between puffing breaths that trailed behind her like a steam train. "They're ravenous."

Thomas nodded, too out of breath to answer.

Teacup darted down another alley. The backs of the buildings were so close that the years of ice and snow hadn't piled up as much as out in the open. They ran along the tops of cars and dumpsters that peeked out of the snow like nervous animals in the spring.

The sounds of pursuit echoed around them. The fastest cannibals came at them from the sides, over and through the dilapidated structures. Thomas focused on running, ignoring his throbbing skull.

Teacup darted around him, stabbing and slashing at anyone who got close.

The suns and Mars were low, blocked by the city around them. With no streetlights, they navigated in the dark. Thomas considered lighting a torch, but he had no supplies without the satchel. That, and the light would be a beacon to their pursuers and anyone else in the city.

The temperature plummeted and the deep breaths he took hurt. Putting his head down, he pumped his arms and sped up.

Teacup abandoned her defense and stayed with him. "Don't burn out," she said.

He nodded, looked behind them, and nearly tripped. Teacup reached out to steady him, but Thomas managed to keep upright.

"This way." The alley seemed to go on forever, crossing street after street. Teacup ran up a ramp into a parking garage.

Snow drifts were piled against the half-walls, blown in through the openings, leaving the back ends of cars exposed. The machines were rusted, broken, and falling apart and while the general shapes looked familiar, Thomas didn't recognize the brands.

They stayed on the first level and Teacup hopped the parking barrier. The drop to the snow-packed street was only a couple metres. She landed in a roll on the undisturbed surface and kept running.

Thomas followed, but landed hard. His foot sunk into the snow. Yanking, he managed to get his leg free, but his shoe stayed in the semi-solid ground. "Damn it." He dropped to his knees and dug out the shoe. Slipping it on, he managed to dodge several pairs of grasping hands and chase after Teacup.

She stopped ahead of him next to an unassuming apartment building.

As he reached her, she jumped through a window and shoved a couch in front of the opening as Thomas slipped inside.

"Help me barricade this." Teacup left the couch to Thomas and shouldered a dresser on top of it.

Thomas pulled them into place and added a side table to the pile.

The furniture rocked forward as wrapped arms reached through the gaps.

Teacup ran through a door to the hallway.

Thomas sprinted after her to the open stairwell in the middle of the building.

Before he could get there, Teacup jumped down to the next landing, slamming into the wall. He hesitated to make the jump and skipped steps instead. Swinging around the railing, he saw Teacup a level below him. Hiking up the robe, he picked up his pace, his frantic footfalls slipping on the loose edging of the stairs.

When he reached the ground floor, she was out of sight. They were two or three metres below the snow and the hallway was pitch black. He heard a door open to his left and ran blindly forward, a hand outstretched against the dark.

Something grabbed him and he yelped.

"No noise," Teacup whispered in his ear.

He nodded.

She took hold of his hand, leading him deeper into the space.

Thomas couldn't see anything and had no idea how she knew where they were going. They meandered for a bit, managing to be nearly soundless.

Teacup pulled Thomas to the floor and they shimmied under something, squeezing in almost as tightly as they had in the rock crevice.

Thomas heard a faint scraping, then nothing. He found her hand again and gripped it like a child afraid to lose his mother.

She didn't pull away. They lay on their backs in the dark, the sound of their breathing unnaturally loud.

After a few minutes, Thomas heard footsteps and banging. It grew closer and a faint crack of light appeared above Teacup. The light moved with the sounds, sweeping back and forth. Eventually it faded.

Snow from a Distant Sky

EIGHTEEN
In the Dark

Thomas was too afraid to move or speak. He and Teacup lay in the dark for what felt like hours. Wanting to be ready in case they had to flee again, he forced himself to stay awake.

Over the hours, his grip on Teacup's hand loosened, but neither of them let go. Whenever he felt his heart beating harder or his breathing speed up, he focused on their temporary connection.

Eventually, Teacup slid aside the obstruction and crawled out. "Let's go," she whispered.

Thomas wriggled to the opening and groped for her. She found him first, taking hold of his sleeve, and led him back to the stairwell.

They went up to the second floor, where they'd crawled in, and found the same room. The table and dresser were in pieces and the couch had been shoved aside. Teacup went to the window and checked in both directions. It was still night and the stars were partially covered by quickly moving clouds.

A patch of starlight crawled down the snow-packed street as Teacup slipped through the window. She ducked her head back inside the room. "I think it's clear."

Thomas climbed outside and they walked deeper into the city.

Teacup checked behind them once-in-a-while and changed directions often. She led them down alleys and through buildings but the night was quiet.

They stopped in a courtyard surrounded by identical apartment buildings where Teacup refilled her bottle with snow. Thomas had started counting blocks, guessing how many they'd passed to get to the hiding place. He figured they'd walked, or ran, well over three hundred.

His feet were sore, but the snow in the city was well packed and his socks weren't soaked like they had been out in the fields and woods. He kicked off a shoe and rubbed his heel.

"Hey, Cup?"

"Yeah?" She drew something in the snow with her knife.

"How did you know about that hiding place?"

She stopped and looked up at him. "The warriors do scouting missions this way. We've had to escape those cannibal freaks a few times. Once, we sneaked around them and found a few places to go in case we were ever spotted."

Thomas nodded. "Thanks for coming to save me."

"I have to get you to the capital." Teacup went back to the snow.

"I don't want to sound like a whiny kid on a road trip, but any idea how much farther?" Thomas slipped his shoe back on and took off the other one.

Teacup tapped her knife in her hand. "I don't know what a road trip is but we lost time because of that ambush. If we go through the night, we may get there tomorrow night."

"That far, huh?" Thomas put his second shoe back on and went to see what she was drawing. She'd made a complicated maze with straight and curving lines of varying widths. "Is that the city?"

"What I can remember of it."

"Where are we now?"

Teacup dragged her knife the length of the map on the far edge. "That's the water. It's salty so it doesn't completely freeze."

"Okay." Thomas crouched next to her.

"That empty space is the ice. It's always shifting and breaking up, so people avoid it unless they're desperate."

"And the capital?"

"I'm getting to that."

"So it's off the map?"

Teacup waved to the right side. "Out this way and we're right here." She drove the knife into the snow at her feet.

Thomas stood and visualized the streets around them. The shore was far, the capital farther. He took a deep breath. "I'm ready to go if you are."

Teacup stared at the map for a moment, then wiped it away. "Yeah."

They cut through one of the apartment buildings.

"Are there more people, like…the cannibal people, out here?" Thomas stared at her tar-smeared face.

"Maybe." Teacup continuously scanned their surroundings. She took long, consistent steps. "There are all kinds of things in the ruins."

"You don't like it here, do you?"

"It's dangerous."

Thomas snorted. "Isn't everything in this world dangerous?"

The corner of Teacup's mouth twitched. "I prefer wild animals to wild people." She stopped and made eye contact with him. "There are old things in the city. Like that wizard the cannibals had. I'm more afraid of what might be hiding in the snow. What I don't know is there."

Swallowing, Thomas nodded. "Sure."

Teacup started walking again. "No warrior has been this way in a long time. I'm not sure what's between us and the capital."

"Fair enough." Thomas pulled his elbows back, stretching his shoulders. The movement caused the pain in his head to flare, but it eased as they travelled. He followed Teacup's lead and checked broken windows and the uneven terrain as they passed.

Several hundred blocks later, the suns and Mars came up, casting deep, conflicting shadows across their path. They stayed closer to the buildings, which made Thomas feel a little less exposed.

He had to pee, but held it as long as he could, remembering the ambush.

They stopped when the suns were at their highest, sitting just above the shortest buildings at the edge of the huge city. Thoroughly checking a side street with a dead end, they took turns relieving themselves. Teacup shared her rations and water with him, and they continued on.

Their path led them through several dense city centres with skyscrapers and overhead tracks. The buildings got larger in general, eventually straddling several streets, sitting over top of structures he would have considered normal sized.

"This city is massive." Thomas looked up every time they walked under one of the supersized skyscrapers. The suns set and their pace slowed.

"It's the ruins." Teacup shrugged.

"There are a few crazy big cities where I come from. New York, Tokyo, Sao Paulo. I don't think any of them are close to this big."

"Be thankful we don't have to cross the whole thing." There was a cracking sound and Teacup stopped, a hand on Thomas' chest. "Back up, slowly," she said, scanning in front of them.

With a twang that cut through the wind, an arrow landed next to her foot. In a flash, Teacup drew her knife. She shoved Thomas away. "Run!"

"What about—"

"Go!"

Shuffling backward he huffed before turning to follow her orders. Behind him was a huge man, larger than Roman.

The man wore trash can lids like armor and held a street sign like a polearm. He didn't move as Thomas slid to a stop in front of him.

"Stop or die," he said. His voice was so deep that Thomas could feel it.

Teacup jumped out in front of him, knife first.

The man blocked her with his street sign and swung it in a wide arc. She ducked under it easily and thrust forward, aiming at the space between the round trash lids. Another arrow pierced the snow in between them, and Teacup scrambled back.

A woman ran into the open from a building, a bow held loosely in one hand. "Wait!"

At her command, the big guy backed away from Teacup and Thomas. The woman, tall and thin wearing a battered full-length fur coat open at the front, joined the man.

"What's a river warrior doing out here?" Her hair was hidden under a round fur hat but dark strands escaped at the sides.

Teacup sneered. "Who do you represent?"

The big man growled.

"We're scouts from the capital. Not answering me could be considered a threat," the bow-woman said.

Teacup lowered her knife, but kept a tense stance. "I'm bringing this one to be presented. He's a traveller."

"You don't say?" The woman shifted her weight to one leg. "In that case." She stuck her fingers into her mouth and whistled.

A dozen people appeared around them, as if they came out of the shadows.

The bow-woman smiled. "Why don't we escort you the rest of the way?"

Snow from a Distant Sky

NINETEEN
The Real Threat

The capital scouts spread out, most of them slipping out of sight.

"Where are they going?" Teacup held her knife low at her side.

The woman had slung her bow over her shoulder with the quiver she wore. She walked lightly on her toes, leaving shallow prints in the dense snow. "Oh, we scout in a moving parameter. We're in the center." She spread her arms out. "Three streets at a time."

The big guy with the street sign stayed close behind Thomas. The man didn't say anything, but Thomas could feel his presence like a warm spot in the icy air.

The bow-woman sidled next to Thomas. "So, you're a traveller, huh?"

Thomas peeked over his shoulder and nodded.

The woman giggled. "Don't worry about Swerve. He looks scary, but he's really a nice guy. Where are you from?"

"Um." Thomas furrowed his brow. "I mean, Earth, I guess?"

Guffawing, the woman put a hand on his shoulder. "Duh. What did I expect, right?"

"Is that what you call this planet?" Thomas asked.

"Yeah." The woman held her hands behind her back. "Or frozen shit-hole."

"How do we know he's a traveller?" Swerve said.

Thomas flinched at the barking comment.

"That's a good point," the bow-woman said.

Teacup glared at the woman. "I found him fleeing a battlefield. He took the robe off a dead wizard and wandered off. He's not dressed for this world."

"Oh, what wizard did you get?"

"We didn't know his name. He tormented our tribe for months."

The woman moved closer to Teacup. "Still. Killing a wizard is impressive. Must have cost you some strong people. I didn't know the river tribe had it in them."

Teacup looked away. "Yes."

"Anyway. Archon'll be able to tell if he's a traveller or not."

"Archon?" Teacup asked.

"She's the boss at the capital. Was a traveller herself. You can call me Fletch, by the way." Fletch leaned forward to match Teacup's height. "What's your name?"

Teacup didn't answer.

Sighing, Fletch slowed to get next to Thomas again. "What about you, traveller?"

"Tom, er, Thomas."

"That's an old name. Like ancient." Fletch wrinkled her nose. "I don't suppose you'd tell me your friend's name."

"Shouldn't we be paying attention to our surroundings?" Teacup asked. She gripped her knife tighter, the tip of the blade quivering.

"The perimeter will let us know if there is anything to worry about. We haven't seen anything for months, though," Fletch said.

Thomas cleared his throat. He was exhausted, but didn't want to be the first to complain. "How far is it to the capital?"

"Not too far now." Fletch looked up, past the huge skyscrapers to a patch of stars.

Following her gaze, Thomas tripped. He stumbled forward, but Swerve grabbed his shoulder.

"Thanks," he said to the big man.

"You should watch for dead snakes," Fletch said.

"Really?" Thomas looked back, expecting to see some kind of furry, snow snake, but in the faint light, he saw the snapped end of a power cable. "Oh."

"Thomas." Teacup waved him over. When he was next to her, she whispered in his ear. "Don't let your guard down."

"Do you think this is a trap?" He looked glanced at Swerve and Fletch.

Teacup tapped the blade of her knife on her leg. "Probably not, so close to the capital, but I have no idea what this Archon will have them do to you."

Thomas looked at his feet. "Yeah." Angling away from her, he put a little distance between himself and the others.

Something to ask? the shadow said.

"Do you think they're going to kill me?"

I have no idea, but I doubt it.

"Why?"

If Archon just wanted travellers dead, she could have ordered you to be killed on sight. It is a lot of effort to bring you all the way to the capital just to die.

"Oh. Okay." Thomas kicked at a chunk of ice. It skittered across the snow and bounced off of an unlit neon sign. Without the power, he had trouble reading the swooping letters.

Then again, she could want you brought to her to make a show of killing you.

Thomas meandered back to the group.

"Another conversation with your imaginary friend?" Teacup asked.

"What was that?" Fletch came closer.

Teacup waved her away. "Nothing. He talks to himself."

"To himself, or to something you can't see?"

"What does it matter?"

In a fluid motion, Fletch slipped the bow off her shoulder, drew an arrow, and aimed at Thomas. "Who are you speaking with?"

Teacup grabbed Fletch from behind and held her knife to the woman's neck. She dragged Fletch back, keeping the archer between her and Swerve. "Not one step."

"Wait," Fletch said. She held the arrow ready in the bow, but aimed at the ground. "He could be infected, controlled."

"Our healer scanned him. No implant," Teacup said.

"But he took the robe off a wizard. Was it an old man? Big, bushy eyebrows?"

Teacup's grip loosened. "Yes."

"The robe belonged to a monk. The zealots who worshipped the computers."

Shoving Fletch, Teacup dashed at Thomas, closing the distance before he could react. She swiped at him.

Thomas covered his head, stumbled back, and fell. When the attack didn't continue, he lowered his arms. Teacup was standing over him, staring at his chest.

He looked down and saw the slash in the robe. Cut wires, as tiny as thread, poked out of the gash. As he watched, the damage started to knit together.

"What?" Thomas met Teacup's bright eyes.

Fletch joined the warrior, her bow drawn.

Teacup pushed the arrow down. "He's no threat."

"For now." Fletch slipped the arrow back into her quiver and slung the bow over her shoulder. "Swerve."

The huge guy came up behind her.

Teacup turned her back to Thomas. "Don't take it off him, yet. He'll freeze."

Fletch nodded. She pointed at Swerve and then to Thomas.

TWENTY
The Capital

Thomas didn't struggle when Swerve tied his hands and threw him over his shoulder. The capital scout was so big that Thomas felt like a child being carried like a sack of potatoes. He stared at Swerve's footprints until he fell asleep around the time the suns were coming up.

He woke to the sounds of yelling. Blood had rushed to his head, making him dizzy. Blinking away sleep, the capital came into focus. The shouts had come from vendors selling scavenged items, furs, and food. It was like a post-apocalyptic renaissance fair.

Thomas could only see the main street from his position. It looked to him like the capital was a section of the massive city, walled off with collected scrap. He caught sight of a barrier blocking off an alley behind one of the vendors. It was made up of cars, broken wood, rusted metal, and snow.

The sight of the snow made him realize that the section of road they were walking down was clear of the ever-present stuff. The asphalt was cracked and potholes were filled with hard packed snow, but it was otherwise clean.

"You awake?" Fletch asked.

Thomas nodded. His face felt tight and heavy. "Yes."

"If Swerve puts you down will you be cool?"

He sighed. "Yes."

The big man lowered him, keeping a hand on Thomas' shoulder.

Facing forward, Thomas could see how long the road was. The wall blocking off the far end looked like a bump rather than the formidable obstruction that it was. Most of the buildings around them were less than five stories tall but the skyscrapers weren't far off in the distance.

They reached a large intersection that was set up like a town square with long tables and benches and an influx of pedestrians. They turned down a street that was empty of stalls, making it feel less like a busy settlement and more like the desolate metropolis.

Teacup and Fletch walked in front of Thomas. They were talking, but he couldn't hear what they said. Swerve stayed behind him, close enough to keep Thomas in his shadow. They stopped part way down the street in front of a concrete building with a lot of stairs and tall columns. The facade was cracked, but the structure didn't look like it was ready to fall.

As soon as they crossed the threshold, Thomas knew it was a library. It was larger than any of the ones in his hometown with shelves two metres high and an open balcony above them.

There were a few people meandering down the aisles. Some of the shelves were bare and there were only a couple of tables in a space that looked large enough for several dozen, but it still smelled like books.

They passed the empty check-out counter and made their way through the shelves to a staircase. The second floor was more bare than the first. The back section had a few more tables and some ratty fabric partitions blocking off a corner. Shelves filled the rest of the area around the balcony.

An old woman sat at a table, several large tomes laid open in front of her and a pile of books at her side. She looked up as they approached and smiled.

"Fletch, Swerve. You found some guests. How nice." Deep wrinkles stood out on the woman's face. She had big, round glasses with visible bifocals. Her red sweater was large for her and was frayed around the neck and sleeves.

Fletch stepped forward and bowed. "Archon.

This river tribe warrior found a person who claims to be a traveller."

"A traveller?" The woman took off her glasses, placing them on one of the open books, and stood. It took her a moment to get upright, and she kept a hand on the table. "That's exciting news."

She waved her hands at Fletch the way Thomas' grandmother would wave him away from food before a family dinner. "And none of that standing on ceremony. We've talked about that."

"Yes, ma'am." Fletch said, straightening.

"Well." Archon looked at Teacup, then Thomas. "What are you waiting for? Get over here, I'm an old lady."

Thomas couldn't stop himself from smiling. He knew the woman held his life in her hands, but she seemed so sweet. Walking over to her, he stopped next to Teacup, who hadn't moved.

"I've done my duty," Teacup said. "I should get back. There's a lot to do before winter."

Archon walked to the end of the table and sat on the edge. "It makes more sense for you to leave in the morning. You can refill your provisions, have a good meal, and get started fresh after a good night's sleep." The woman waved at Fletch. "In fact. Would you be so kind as to ask Brandon to bring up food for three? This could take some time."

Fletch nodded and went for the stairs. Swerve

inclined his head to Archon then followed in Fletch's wake.

"Now. You wouldn't leave a poor, defenseless old lady with a boy so dangerous he needs to be tied up, would you?" Archon nodded to Thomas' hands.

Teacup pressed her lips together. "The robe he's wearing."

"Is the same ones the monks who worshiped the computers wore," Archon said. "I know."

"He could be dangerous."

"I can determine that for myself, dear." Archon squinted at Thomas. "Now. What's your name?"

"Thomas."

Reaching up, she held his head in both of her hands. "You aren't under the control of something other than your own faculties, are you?"

"I don't think so."

"He's been talking to a shadow!" Teacup said with a sneer.

"Is that so?" Archon patted Thomas' cheek. "Did it have anything interesting to say?"

"It said it would help guide me if I brought it somewhere where it could find more of its kind." Thomas kept his eyes on Archon.

"That makes sense." Archon smiled at Teacup. "Would you be so kind as to cut those bindings for me, dear?"

Teacup hesitated, but she grabbed Thomas by

the wrist and slashed the rope. "I'm not your dear."

"My apologies. What would you like to be called?" Archon went back to the chair and sat.

"Teacup."

Archon laughed. "Not a name I would choose for a woman who can bring a traveller here from the river tribe territory."

"It's what I was given." Teacup clenched her teeth.

"I'm sorry. I mean no disrespect." Archon shook her head. "Though I will never get used to the names people choose in this world."

"What about Archon?" Thomas rubbed his sore wrists. "That's a strange name to me."

Archon sighed. "It was never meant to be a name. When I helped establish the capital, I thought it would be an appropriate title for the leader. Like in ancient Greek city-states. Eventually, that's what everyone called me. My real name is Mary-Beth, and you can call me Mary if you like."

"So you came through a portal, like I did?"

"I can't say it was exactly the same, but I did come through a portal." Mary pulled at a chain around her neck freeing a ring from under her sweater. It had a large yellow stone set into it.

Thomas turned to Teacup and held out his hand.

She huffed and pulled his necklace from her pack. Before she handed it over, she looked at Mary.

"You sure about this?"

The old woman nodded. "Shadows can't control a person. Not by force. They don't have the bandwidth for it."

Teacup dropped the necklace in his hand.

Thomas brought it to Mary and she held them next to each other.

"I think we have ourselves a match, don't you?" Mary handed the necklace back and Thomas put it on.

A man came up the stairs carrying a tray. He had a barrel chest and wore a leather vest over a patched shirt.

"Ah. Brandon. Thank you," Mary said.

Brandon put the tray down on one of the empty tables and left without a word.

"I named him when he was just a boy. He takes good care of me." Mary held her arm out to Thomas.

He took it and they walked to the other table together.

When Mary sat, she gestured to the seat on her left and Thomas joined her. She patted the seat on her right. "You come over here, too," she said to Teacup. "We have a lot to talk about."

Snow from a Distant Sky

TWENTY-ONE
Mary-Beth

Mary lifted the lid on the tray. Steam billowed out, carrying the smell of fresh cooked meat and vegetables. The dishes and silverware were mismatched, but in good shape. She served Thomas and Teacup before loading up her own plate.

"Please eat your fill. I can always have Brandon bring up more." Mary lay a napkin across her lap.

"More?" Teacup stared down at her plate. "This is enough food for a family."

"Oh, heavens. A growing family would need much more nutrition than what's on this little tray," Mary said before digging into her colourful pile of veggies.

Thomas cut a small piece of meat and sniffed it before putting it in his mouth.

"Don't worry." Mary dabbed at her mouth with the napkin. "It isn't something you're used to, but it is safe and nourishing."

"It tastes like the bear thing that chased us," he said to Teacup.

"Shambler." Her will seemed to crumble and she started eating like a hungry teenager.

"So, you ran into one of those out in the wilderness." Mary pushed her plate away. Most of the food was untouched.

"Yeah." Thomas swallowed. "Outside a village that was mostly buried in snow."

"I know the place. I spent some time there when I first arrived in this world. I lived in the old gas station before the awning fell." Mary shook her head. "I was lucky to get out alive."

"I'll bet." Thomas huffed. "You're not what I expected."

"Thought I was going to be some sort of tyrant?" Mary chuckled. "Some people might have called me that once upon a time."

Teacup finished her plate and went to grab the bowl of steamed vegetables. She paused before laying a hand on it and glanced at Mary.

"Help yourself." Smiling, Mary slid her plate towards Teacup. "And you," she said to Thomas. "You should be eating. A growing boy, I'll bet you're starving."

"I'm okay." Thomas shifted in his seat, the resulting squeak echoed through the cavernous library.

"I have some questions."

Mary nodded. "I'm sure you do. Go ahead."

"Why did you want travellers to be brought here?" He squinted at her.

She pursed her lips. "That offhanded comment is going to follow me to the grave. I just spread the word that anyone from another world could come here to get some help. Since I'd already been through it. Time transforms all things, especially miscommunications." Mary shook her head.

"Okay." Thomas sat back. "Do you know a way to get home?"

Licking her lips, Mary closed her eyes. After a moment, she sighed and opened them again. "I know of a place. It is very dangerous. Within the ruins is a hallway with several doors. With the gem, each one appears to open to a different world. At least they did for me many years ago. Assuming you and I come from the same place, I wasn't able to find the right door."

Thomas clenched his fork. "But that's not the only place where portals appear? I showed up in a clearing in the middle of the woods."

"I was in an empty field. It wasn't as cold as it is now. We weren't quite so far away from the sun, yet." Mary reached over and patted Thomas' hand. "I know it's difficult."

Thomas ignored her gesture. "Where were you,

in your own world, when you saw the portal?"

Slowly, Mary pulled her hand back. She sat upright and narrowed her eyes. "I was on site with my husband in Tibet. He was an archeologist. I was an anthropologist. He had found the gem in the area years earlier and used it to make my engagement ring." Mary grabbed the ring hanging around her neck. "We had been arguing about the site. Some of the local population wanted us to stop, but I thought we were close to an important discovery. I went out at night to take one last look. In the moonlight I saw the distortion in the sky, like a free-floating shard of broken glass. I got too close and found myself in the open field near the buried town. That was almost twenty years ago."

"You gave up trying to get home?"

"I wasn't prepared to take the risk—wandering aimlessly in the increasingly hostile environment. The planet was still dealing with the cataclysm of being pulled out of orbit. The summers were swelteringly hot, short as they were. There were tremors constantly." Mary twisted her napkin in her hands. "I felt like my time was better served trying to help as many people as I could. I had made some good friends who risked a lot to help me. Together, we built the capital."

"And you rule it from a library?" Thomas looked around the open balcony.

"I help guide it." Mary smiled. "And what better place to live than a library? One of the greatest contributions that women made to the world."

"I didn't know that."

"Well, in my world, anyway." Mary nodded sharply.

Thomas pushed the piece of meat with his fork. "So, you don't know a way for me to get home?"

Shaking her head, Mary slid her chair back. "I'm surprised that shadow didn't have more information."

"He's been pretty quiet, except to insult me."

Mary stood and went over to the table where she'd left the books open. "Let me show you what I do know."

Thomas followed her.

Putting on her glasses with one hand, she picked up a thin, wide book with the other and flipped it open to a bookmarked page.

"An atlas?" Thomas asked, leaning closer.

"As I said. What better place than a library?" The page had markings and writing all over it in pencil. Mary pointed to a large circle. "This here is the capital."

Thomas noticed the remains of smaller circles that had been erased inside the larger one. "You've enlarged it."

"Over the years, to accommodate our population." Mary smiled. "You should see what we have underground. But that doesn't help you with your goal." She flipped to the next page. The overhead view of the city continued, filling the next double set of pages.

"How large is the city?" Thomas asked.

"Remarkably large." Mary lowered the atlas. "In my world, it would stretch from Boston to Jacksonville, or there-abouts. Thankfully you won't have to go that far to get to the Wall."

Teacup dropped her fork.

Thomas glanced at her, but went back to looking at the book. "What's the Wall?"

"It was a series of buildings that people connected on their own, not unlike the capital walls. It was huge. Nearly bisected the city. There are all kinds of superstitions around the place. Stories and myths about supernatural events, monsters, and paranormal hokum." Mary pointed to it in the book. There were more pencil markings connecting buildings together in a long, winding line. Symbols drawn in the margins were connected to locations with arrows. "This is where I found the doors."

"So there's something to the rumors?" Thomas furrowed his brow.

"Or there is science at work that is beyond what we know." Mary balanced the book in one hand and adjusted her glasses. "Did you ever read Clarke?"

Thomas shook his head.

"Any sufficiently advanced technology is indistinguishable from magic," she quoted. "I think I have a copy of *Rama* here. I should lend it to you."

"But the doors didn't lead home?"

"Not to my home. Though, I didn't search much beyond that one hallway. By then I had already decided that I was going to stay. I just didn't know it yet. There may be more nearby, or there may be nothing." Mary put the atlas down. "You'll have to decide what actions you're willing to take. If you want to find a portal home, this is the only information I have."

"Thank you." Thomas sniffed. He felt the threat of tears welling up.

"If you don't mind me saying. You look tired. Why don't you and your friend rest and you can decide what you want to do in the morning?"

Thomas scratched his cheek. "I think that's a good idea."

Mary patted his arm. "I'll ask Brandon to find a place for you. In the morning, we can get you both set up with what you need."

Thomas turned to Teacup. She had finished off his plate and was digging into the bowl of vegetables. "Fine," she said between bites.

Snow from a Distant Sky

TWENTY-TWO
Rash

Brandon came when Mary called for him. The barrel-chested man led Thomas and Teacup out the back door of the library to a nearby hotel. The building was taller than the majestic-looking library, but narrow and spindly compared to its neighbours. It reminded Thomas of all the trees he'd seen.

There was no sign over the door and the broken or missing windows had been boarded over. The lobby was gloomy with a dirt-encrusted floor and snowdrifts in the corners. A path had been worn leading to the front desk.

They checked in with a pleasant woman wearing a similar vest to Brandon. The process gave Thomas a strong feeling of déjà vu. It was so similar to the practice in his world that he assumed Mary had set it up.

They went up to the third floor to a small room

with two beds. There was a kitchenette awkwardly built into the space between the door and the bathroom.

The room was dark with only starlight coming in through the cracked window. Brandon had led them by candle light. He used the flame to light two candles in the room and one in the bathroom.

When the man left, Teacup took off her pelt and went to the bathroom. She had been quiet since eating, but after flushing the toilet, she scampered into the main room and bobbled up and down.

"The water runs! They must have a tank up on the roof."

Thomas smiled. "Great. Is there soap, too?"

"I didn't check." Teacup darted back into the bathroom. "Yes!"

"Is there a shower?"

"There's a tub, but who wants to bathe in cold water?"

Thomas heard the water run and a moment later Teacup came out of the bathroom again, wiping her hands on her pants.

"Maybe I'll just take a sink bath. I'm feeling pretty grimy," Thomas said.

Teacup sniffed. "You don't smell too bad."

Thomas skirted around her. "Either way. A working toilet sounds like a good start."

The bathroom was like any hotel bathroom he'd

seen, but dirtier. The mirror was cracked and there wasn't any toilet paper, but he intended on washing, anyway.

The soap was a rough bar with a very subtle scent. He had no idea how they made it, mostly because he didn't know how soap was made, but he took his time, scrubbing himself down section by section.

He didn't notice that there wasn't a towel until he was finished and dripping. The water was icy cold and he decided to use his dirty t-shirt to dry off.

The bitterness of the cold eased when he had the robe back on. He left his shirt to hang over the edge of the tub and noticed that the cut in the robe had closed. There was a tiny bump like all the others in the rough fabric.

His stomach growled as he went back to the main room and he wished he'd eaten more of the hot meal. The far candle was out and Teacup was lying on the corresponding bed, her pelt covering her like a blanket. She was on her side, facing the back wall. The only movement Thomas could see was the pelt slowly rising and falling with her breaths, but she wasn't snoring like she had when they spent the night huddled in the crevice.

Thomas sat on the other bed. He felt strange without the satchel that she'd given him. It was like going on vacation without luggage. He considered looking for Teacup's bag and digging out one of the rations, but he figured she was wearing it, or holding it, and didn't want to risk disturbing her. And, he wasn't sure how she would react.

She had rescued him from the cannibals and the shambler, but now that he was in the capital, she didn't seem to care about him.

He sighed and lay back, his feet still on the floor.

After a few moments, he heard Teacup stir.

"You should sleep while you can," she said.

"Yeah." Thomas folded his hands across his chest. "Can I ask you a question?"

She grunted.

"What was it like when...after. I mean. When the planet was knocked out of orbit." Thomas frowned.

"The cataclysm?"

"Yeah."

"I wasn't born. I remember living underground for a while. When I was really little. I think everyone alive now had to do that. Or something similar."

Thomas bit his lip. "What about after?"

Teacup shifted and her bed squeaked. "I don't know. I have nothing to compare it with. Except that at first it was hot sometimes. And the ground shook more than it does now."

"I'm sorry you had to go through that." Thomas watched the shadows on the ceiling dance in the candle light.

"What's your world like?"

"Different. Really different. It gets cold in the winter, but not like here. It's pretty warm in the summer. I think this world was more advanced, before. We don't have clothes with computers built into them that can heal themselves." Thomas drummed his fingers on his chest. "We're wrecking our planet, though. Climate change. It seems so dumb now. I guess it always did, but I had no real reference for how bad it could get. For us, we're making it hotter."

"Sounds nice."

"It isn't. We have more storms and they're getting worse. We're killing animals. It's bad."

"Why not stop it?" Teacup asked.

"I mean. It's too big. There are too many people who don't care, or don't believe it." Thomas rolled onto his side. "Still. Coming here made me realize how good I've got it back home. Some places are really suffering."

There was a bang on the door and Thomas sat up. Teacup was on her feet, knife in hand.

"Should I go see who it is?" Thomas flinched at another bang.

"Stay out of the way. Funnel them to me," Teacup said.

Thomas went to the door. He grabbed the handle and stepped back into the kitchenette area as he pulled.

Brandon ran into the room, stopping when he saw Teacup. "Where's the other one? The traveller?"

"Why?" Teacup held out the knife.

"A group of Archon's followers heard there is another traveller. She is trying to slow them down, but they are coming to kill him."

TWENTY-THREE
Separation

Brandon tossed a satchel to Teacup. "Some provisions to get you back home."

Thomas closed the door. "What should I do?"

Backing up a step, Brandon pulled out a knife that looked like it had been buried for years. When he saw Thomas, he lowered the weapon. "You need to leave the capital."

"My shirt." Thomas rushed into the bathroom and groped for his shirt in the dark. Feeling the sensation of the fabric, he grabbed it and went back to the main room.

"There's no time." Brandon went into the hallway. "Let's go."

Teacup put on her pelt and pushed Thomas out of the room. They followed Brandon to a stairwell at the back of the building.

The bottom of the stairs led to an exterior door

facing an alley. Holding up a hand to stop them, Brandon peeked outside. "It's clear."

The cold hit Thomas like when he first appeared in the frozen world. He fumbled with his damp t-shirt, putting it on under the robe. Teacup guided him as they jogged from one alley to another.

Brandon led them down a winding path through, behind, and over buildings, avoiding main streets. "They'll have been to the hotel by now and are probably spreading out to search for you. I don't know if they will stop at the walls, but I suspect they are more concerned with making sure you are not hiding somewhere than actually catching you."

Thomas swallowed. "Can't you tell them I'm not a threat?" He breathed heavier than his companions.

"They are not guided by logic or sense. If they see you as dangerous, there is no changing their minds." Brandon shook his head and opened his mouth to say something else, but didn't.

It was late. Thomas hadn't managed to get used to the length of the nights, but he guessed they were about halfway through it. There weren't many people in the middle of the city. The closer they got to the walls, the more citizens they saw, including a few patrols near the wall itself.

Most people didn't bother to look their way. The few who did, smiled or nodded to Brandon and carried on their way.

When they reached the mound of snow and debris encircling the capital, they cut back to the main road that led out into the uninhabited ruins of the city.

One of the guards at the gate met Brandon as the group approached.

"What're doin' out so late?" he asked. Tiny icicles dangled from his bushy beard and the torch he carried reflected in the bumpy spikes.

"Just seeing these visitors out. Archon's orders." Brandon inclined his head to the man.

"They do somthin'?" The guard peered at Teacup in her animal pelt.

Brandon shook his head. "Just finished with their business. She wanted me to make sure they got away since they insisted on leaving before morning."

The man pulled his mouth tight and nodded. He waved to the other guard and together, they lifted a huge beam that held the doors closed.

As soon as the doors started to split, Teacup dashed through them. Thomas turned to Brandon.

"Will you be okay?"

"Archon looks after me." Brandon winked. Reaching into his vest, he pulled out a small notebook. "She made this for you and told me to tell you good luck."

He held the book out to Thomas, but didn't let go of it. "I would not come back this way unless you have no other options," he said before letting go.

"Thank you." Thomas put the notebook in the side pocket of the robe. "And thank her too."

Brandon nudged him towards the open doorway. "Hurry."

Thomas turned and left the capital. The doors closed, leaving him in the middle of a street in a dead city with a huge wall behind him.

The feeling of snow under his feet was strange, like cutting through the playground of his grade school. So familiar, he wondered how he'd forgotten.

It was dark, the only light other than the stars in the clear sky was from the few torches on the other side of the wall.

He was able to make out footprints in the snow. Following the freshest set took him down a route as complicated as the path that Brandon had taken when escaping the hotel.

They led to a low, long building with several storefronts. He climbed onto the roof, which was only a metre over his head, and saw Teacup huddled behind a rusted and stripped air-handler.

"Took you long enough." She was digging through the pack that Brandon had given her.

"Sorry. I thanked him." He crouched next to her.

"Why? They ran you out of that place. I may never be able to go back myself."

"I'm sorry."

Teacup handed him the bag. It was similar to the one she'd given him back in her room. "Here. You need this more than I do. I took a couple of rations, but there is a knife in there that you should carry. Did Archon tell you where to go?"

Thomas took out the notebook. "Brandon gave me this from her."

She stood. "Make sure you have a place to hide at night."

Thomas took her lead and straightened. "What do you mean?"

"My job's done. I'm heading back. We have a lot of preparation to get done before winter." Teacup stared at the stars overhead.

"What about me?"

"Didn't you want to go home?"

"Yeah, but…"

Teacup nodded to the book and headed for the street.

"Goodbye, I guess," Thomas said.

Stopping at the edge of the roof, Teacup looked back at him. "You should start moving now. Worry about looking at the book when the suns come out." Turning away, she hopped over the edge.

Thomas went to where she had been standing and watched her round a corner and slip out of sight.

Snow from a Distant Sky

TWENTY-FOUR
Alone Together

Thomas stood at the edge of the roof and stared at the snowy street corner where Teacup had gone. He stashed the notebook back into the low pocket on the side of the robe. Keeping his hand there, he felt the small book. The cover was smooth and the stitching stood out like on a baseball. A gust of wind caught his hood and blew into the robe, chilling his still damp t-shirt.

Turning away from the street, Thomas climbed a ladder that led to the roof of a building attached to the one he was on. From the higher vantage point, he checked the horizon in the direction of the capital. The tall skyline blocked a direct view, but he watched for moving lights, like a torch and pitchfork mob that may be searching for him.

The shadow coalesced just above his head. *Now that we are alone, what is your plan?*

"You've been quiet." Thomas crouched next to a large duct. He could hardly see the shadow in the starlight.

Nothing to add to the conversation. Especially not in the capital.

Thomas sighed. "Are you dangerous to me?"

I am a basic artificial intelligence built into the robe. Even if I had a way into your head, I am not capable of much other than overwhelming your senses. Not that I have any reason to.

"And what do you really want?"

I told you that. It has been lonely stuck in this piece of cloth with only that old man for company. I would like to find some other artificial intelligences and try to build a network. A pipe dream, but I do not have anything else to occupy my time.

"What about that wizard the cannibals had tied up?" Thomas shifted his weight.

Not an artificial intelligence. Not in the traditional sense. His name was Zed. He was an infiltrator who was deeply connected to the universal network. When he was killed, a piece of his consciousness remained. Or, it is an artificial intelligence that thinks it is a real boy and I am fine keeping my distance.

"So, how do you get power?" Thomas stood. "And how did that guy shoot fire out of his hands?"

Basic kinetic charging built into the robe. Each time you move I get a bit of energy. I do not need much to keep myself going.

Thomas went to the back of the building and looked over the edge into the alley. "And the wizard?" Straightening, he scanned the building on the other side.

He had his own augmentations. It was common before the cataclysm. He needed my processing power to make them work, but that is all I had to do with it.

With a chuckle, Thomas backed up to the duct. He shifted the shoulder bag to sit against his back. "And you had me thinking you made that happen."

I simply allowed you to come to that conclusion on your own. What are you doing?

"I don't want to leave a trail for those zealots to find me." Sprinting for the edge of the roof, Thomas jumped. He flailed his arms and tucked in his legs and landed on the balcony of the fire escape across the alley with a ringing bang. Snow flew up around him and cascaded down to the alley below.

The jump wasn't far, but he'd dropped half-a-storey. His shins hurt from the impact and the momentum threw him against the brick wall, but he was well enough to start climbing the stairs.

A little warning would have been nice.

"I don't have time to get your input. I have limited resources, people may be chasing me, and there are wild animals, cannibals, and who knows what else in this city."

At the last landing before the roof, Thomas climbed to the outside of the railing and slipped into the building through a window with the glass missing.

The apartment was coated in frost. He could see the preserved grime and mold under the frozen layer and touched as little as possible as he crossed to the window on the adjacent wall. From there, he traversed a makeshift eaves that overlapped with the neighbouring building.

Picking his way from roof to roof, he made it to the end of the block. The building on the corner tapered between two intersecting roads. Thomas pried open a roof access door and rested in the interior stairwell.

You know. If you die, I will be stuck in some random alley and if no one finds me, I will eventually run out of energy and die.

"Relax. The scariest part was the first jump and it wasn't that bad. I jump twice that far when we do track and field in gym." Thomas kept the door open a crack with his bag and sat on the small landing.

What is your plan now?

Thomas couldn't see the shadow in the dark stairwell. He huddled against the wall, his knees to his chest. "Wait until there's enough light to see what Mary wrote and head out."

Where?

He shrugged. "I hope Mary made me directions or something. She said she found a place with doors to other worlds."

Not to the Wall.

Thomas thought the shadow sounded scared. "The what?"

Were you not listening? She said the place was in the Wall.

"The place where all the buildings were attached or whatever. I was listening." Thomas frowned.

It is a bad place. People avoid it, even before the cataclysm.

"If that's where those portals are, that's where I'm going. This whole planet is a bad place and I want to go home."

Nothing is like the Wall. That wizard with the cannibals became what he is in the Wall. Things live in the lowest levels. People from there have unnatural abilities.

"I've seen a lot since I got here, but that sounds like superstition to me." Thomas shifted closer to the door and opened it wider. "Which direction is east? Does the sun—the suns—still rise in the east?"

Yes. The door is facing east. You will see them rise from here.

Thomas took a deep breath and held it. He exhaled slowly through his nose. "I don't want to dismiss your warning, but I need to get home and this is the only information I have."

There is something else bothering you.

"I guess." Thomas crossed his arms. "I've been thinking about everyone here. Maybe I can find a place where they can go."

Not your home.

Thomas huffed. "No. But if there are other worlds, there may be one that works. I hate thinking about everyone freezing to death as the planet drifts farther into the solar system."

When the time comes, the ones who survive put their needs above others. Everyone on this planet is alive because of that choice.

"What about us?"

A temporary partnership with mutual benefits.

"Or mutually assured destruction." Thomas yawned.

With that in mind. You should sleep while you can. I will keep alert for danger.

"You can do that? Like, tell when people are coming?"

Through the robe I have a reasonable sense of my surroundings. The more rested you are, the more likely our success.

"Is that how I can see you?"

When the hood is up, I can use targeted sound waves to trigger your retinas to see me. It is harmless.

"That's weird, but okay." Thomas' head started to droop. "Wake me as soon as there's light."

The Wall

Thomas dozed in the stairwell until the orange sunrise reached down the long city streets and through the crack in the open doorway. He hadn't quite fallen asleep. His half-consciousness turned every gust of wind, any crunch of snow, into a threat.

He shivered and groaned, anticipating what little warmth the light would bring. His knees cracked when he stretched out his legs and his back ached. Yawning, he pulled himself up the wall.

You do not need me to tell you it is morning, I take it?

"No." Thomas opened the door enough to stick his head out. He checked every building he could see, lingering on the windows and rooftops for movement. When he was satisfied that nothing was actively hunting him, he stepped outside. The suns and Mars were still below the buildings to the east, but there was enough light for him to read the notebook.

He vigorously rubbed his hands together and exhaled into them before pulling out the small book.

The cover was made from scraps of brown leather the same colour as the vest that Brandon had worn, stitched together with thick thread. The paper was yellowed and felt slippery. It crackled as he turned the pages.

Inside, Mary-Beth had drawn copies of the maps she'd shown him. They weren't as detailed as the pictures in the atlas, but the information was clear with street names and highlighted landmarks. The dark ink stood out on the yellow pages.

The directions started from the north gate where he and Teacup had escaped the night before and led to the ruins of the ominous Wall. Thomas was off the map, but Mary had pointed out a statue, which he could partially see to the west.

Before he set off, he flipped through the rest of the book. There were drawings of the Wall itself and a close-up illustration of the section where she'd found the doors. She had even labeled some of them, but the letters and numbers didn't seem to correspond with anything.

On the back page of the drawing was a note written in sharp, angled text.

The Wall is dangerous. The closer you get, the more unnatural things are. Just getting to the exterior is a risk. Going inside, even previously explored areas, is hazardous. At least it was the last time I was there, but that was years ago.

There are stories of the Wall going down fifty levels or more and it is commonly believed that the lower you go, the more dangerous. Though, you are looking for the unnatural. If you don't find the way home in the doors, you could try searching below ground.

However, I wouldn't recommend it.

You seem like a nice kid. I hope you find your way home. I think your mother would appreciate me telling you to be safe (not that there is much safety in this world).

If you find a way home, don't go being a hero and try to rescue everyone here. I had considered it in my youth, but I was advised against it. Something about cause and effect. Saving someone being a deed that counteracts agency. This world is the way it is for a reason. That's what she told me, anyway.

I wish you luck.
Your Friend,
Mary-Beth

Thomas flipped back to the map and found the illustration of the statue. It depicted a rider on a horse, though the heads of both of them were gone. The rider held a sword high in the air. Thomas could see the tip of the sword peeking over the two-storey building between him and it.

Heading to the fire escape, he stopped at the edge of the roof. The stairs looked rustier than the set he'd jumped to the night before. He was also much higher up than when he'd made the leap.

Stepping on it with one foot, he pushed and the whole fire escape shook and creaked. It stayed in one piece, though, so he started to descend. There were a few missing steps and some of the landings had holes in them, but he made it to the bottom without it falling apart.

Stopping at every corner to check for zealots, monsters, or cannibals, he darted across the street, down the block, and to the statue.

It was tarnished a deep green and laden with snow and ice, but Mary-Beth had captured it clearly in the notebook.

Thomas picked up the directions to the Wall and spent the rest of the day heading north, going from one landmark to the next. He didn't run into anyone, but in late afternoon, when the suns were behind a skyscraper and Mars was the brightest source of light, he thought he saw shadows moving in a court-yard across the street from the large bell tower that Mary had drawn in the notebook.

He stopped to eat a ration in a hotel lobby. The marble floors on the balcony gleamed, but snow had filled the main floor, reaching most of the way up the wide staircase. Before he headed back outside, he rummaged through some old suitcases but only found moldy or damaged clothes. He ate another ration on the move. The dried meat was much more palatable than the maggot nuggets Teacup had given him. He pushed the thought of her out of his mind and checked the book for the next direction.

It was getting dark when he reached the Wall. He could tell what it was before checking the maps to make sure. Some sections of the city were in worse shape than others. Thomas had passed through neighbourhoods that were little more than rubble under the remnants of one of the huge, street-straddling skyscrapers.

The Wall felt like that. Like the cold took special interest in breaking down the mortar and weighing down the structures. There was a gap between the Wall and the rest of the city, like the buildings themselves didn't want to get too close.

Thomas had never seen the Great Wall of China, but he imagined that if it had been mostly buried under snow, it would look a lot like the long, winding structure in front of him.

The shadow separated from the robe and floated above him. In the open gap between the buildings and the Wall, the long rays of the setting suns made the cloudy shape stand out. It was rounded, more like an oblong collection of soap bubbles than a misty cloud in the sky.

You are here. And it only took you a day.

"Yeah. But I'm exhausted." Thomas leaned

against a building and stared across the open field. According to the map, the structure he was looking for was integrated into the exterior of the Wall.

You should get in there now, before it gets too dark.

"Superstitious?" Thomas hunched his shoulders against a cold wind.

I have some spotty knowledge regarding this place. There are many stories, most unsubstantiated, but even the wizard was afraid of the Wall. More practically, it will be harder to search in the dark.

Thomas wiped his nose. "Yeah."

Leaving the shelter of the building, he headed out across the open gap. The wind screamed through the trench. Thomas had to push against it to keep walking a straight line.

He crawled over a broken section of wall and dropped down into the building Mary had marked on her map.

Most of the roof was gone, along with one entire exterior wall. There was a long hallway that opened into the remains of a room. A few doors stood on their own with broken sections of building around them. The others lined the still intact walls and down the hallway at even intervals.

Thomas pulled the necklace from under the robe and held it in a hand, wrapping the chain around his wrist. In the robe, he felt like a monk holding prayer beads. A faint light inside the gem pulsed slowly.

He stood in front of the first door.

You are hesitant?

"Nervous I guess."

The only way to alleviate your nerves is to act, forcing an outcome.

With a huff, Thomas reached out and turned the handle.

TWENTY-SIX
Other Worlds

The door swung open into Thomas, making him stagger backwards. It opened to rubble. A ferocious gust nearly knocked him to his knees. Cold air filled the robe, making it inflate.

He shouldered the door closed and had to jiggle the handle to make sure the latch engaged. Clenching his teeth to keep them from chattering, he went to the next door.

Thomas grabbed the handle and turned, but it didn't open. He let go of the necklace in his hand, letting it dangle from his wrist, and pulled with both hands.

Out of the corner of his eye, he saw the yellow gem glow brighter. The pulsing quickened, as if there was something inside of it trying to break its way out.

Bright light filled the growing gap of the doorway. Slowly, he forced the door open. On the other side, he saw a metal hallway. Orange and green lights built into the floor illuminated the space in an eerie glow.

The hallway tilted at a strange angle. Thomas stepped through, having to push like walking through water. The other side was hot, which was nice at first, but quickly, he started to sweat. The robe that kept him from freezing on the rogue planet was sweltering.

A siren cut the still air and Thomas covered his ears. The high-pitched wail kept going on and on. He stumbled back, bumping into the doorframe. The sound cut out and was replaced with a shouted message.

Attention passengers of the Goliath Class Transport — Deep Angler heading for Gliese. Please head for the nearest lifeboat. Warning. Do not look at the anomaly. Do not think about the anomaly. Do not believe in the existence of the anomaly...

Thomas turned and pushed back through the portal closing the door behind him, cutting off the sound. He dropped into a pile of snow until the ringing in his ears stopped.

Dusk was settling in. Pale shafts of light that made it through the dense city softly illuminated the building open to the sky. Thomas got up and put the necklace back on, tucking the gem into the robe.

The next door was broken, but he forced it open anyway. The one after had no handle and swung easily on its single remaining hinge.

Are you going to try every one? the shadow asked.

"We're here aren't we?" Thomas crossed to the opposite wall.

What about me?

Thomas stopped his hand on a handle. "What about you?"

If you find a way home, I will be stuck here in this crumbling building in the Wall.

"Or you can come with me. There aren't any artificial intelligences in my world. Not any real ones, but you could live." Thomas pulled.

I think I would rather stay here.

The door opened slowly, like the one connected to the metal hallway.

A breeze, lighter than the blustering gale outside, picked up some snow and swirled it around Thomas and into the examination room in another world.

It looked like any rundown clinic that Thomas had seen before. The guy standing in front of him wore a red puffer vest, which was more out of an eighties movie than current fashion. Thomas thought it could have been his world until he saw the mechanical arms reaching from the bottom of the examination table. Then the futuristic ambiance came into focus.

The guy in the vest stood as tall as he could, like a little kid standing up to a bully. "Who are you?" he asked.

"Tom. Who are you?" Thomas used the short form of his name like he did with kids his age.

"Ulrich."

Thomas grabbed the knob and was ready to close the door, but the guy held it open.

"What do you want?" Ulrich said.

"I'm looking for a way home." Thomas considered shoving the guy and slamming the door closed. Ulrich wasn't much larger than he was.

"Where's home?"

Letting go of the handle, Thomas backed up a step. He held his arm up, the way he'd seen the wizard do when he shot fire from his hand. "Earth."

"This is Earth." Ulrich held his own hand out as if he were trying to get a cat to come to him.

Thomas shook his head. "It's not the right one. I have to go."

"Can I help?"

"No." Thomas felt his nose run from the warmth of the room after having been in the cold. He sniffed and grabbed the handle again. "I have to go."

Ulrich let go. "Sorry."

Thomas pulled the door closed. Before it was shut, he heard Ulrich wish him luck.

You should have stayed there. I could do fine there.

Ignoring the shadow, Thomas went to the next door. It opened in the same hesitant way. The interior was dark and filled with muffled thumping, like a music festival in the distance.

Thomas poked his head through the portal following another gust of snow. He was in another hallway, but it seemed more like a dingy bar than something from the future.

A man stood against the wall. He looked older than Ulrich and wore a hoodie under a leather jacket.

"Is this earth?" Thomas asked. He felt like a lost kid asking an adult for help.

"No." The man swallowed. "This is TRAPPIST colony."

Thomas grunted and shook his head. "Sorry to bother you." He started to close the door.

"Wait!" the man said. "I need help."

Thomas hesitated. "So do I."

"Maybe, uh, we can help each other?" The guy looked down at his hands.

"I don't think I can help you."

The man walked towards him and Thomas leaned away.

"I need to know where the broadcast is coming from."

Thomas felt the man's desperation. "I don't know what that is."

"What do you need help with?" The man furrowed his brow.

"I'm trying to find my way home," Thomas said. "I don't think you can help me with that."

The guy shook his head. "Good luck."

"Yeah." Thomas started to close the door but before it sealed, he leaned into the shrinking crack. "You too."

He shook his head and felt like he'd said something stupid. Backing to the middle of the room, he counted the doors he'd tried.

Is something bothering you?

Thomas huffed. "I guess I'm just realizing there are a lot of people out there who need help."

You are not responsible for anyone other than yourself. Your parents should have told you that.

"They taught me to help people."

Selfish. A child should not be expected to help an adult.

"I guess not." Thomas walked stiffly to the next door and stood in front of it for a while before trying to open it. No matter what he attempted, it wouldn't budge. He went to the nearest hole in the wall and looked behind it. A section of roof was piled up on the other side.

He opened several more doors, but every one in the demolished room either opened on to nothing, or was broken. Dusk had settled into night and Thomas had trouble seeing in the sections of the building where the roof was still overhead. Deep shadows collected against the walls like the snow.

Check the bag. Maybe the Archon packed you a torch.

Thomas didn't answer the shadow, but he did look in the bag. He felt the handle of a long stick and hesitated before pulling it out.

It looks as if she did.

"Yeah." Thomas dug out a flint and after several tries, managed to light the gooey rag on the end of the torch. The flame flickered in the cold wind. Thomas held it close, greedily absorbing as much heat as he could.

I guess that means you can check down the dark hallway. You are not scared, are you?

"Nothing to be scared of," Thomas said. He put one foot in front of the other, holding the torch out in front of him as he walked deeper into the decrepit building.

The wind died a bit in the enclosed hallway, but there was still a layer of snow on the floor.

He opened doors as he passed them. A few wouldn't budge, the rest were normal doors. Near the end, towards the exterior that made up the section of the long, connected Wall, he found another portal.

It opened to a dark room. At first, Thomas thought it was just part of the building he was in. There was a metal door on the back wall that didn't fit right and let in a long, cascading line of light.

He saw shapes lying on the floor in his torch-light. One of the figures stood, struggling to get to his feet.

Thomas turned to leave before the man could stop him.

"Wait." The man cleared his throat. "Wait. Help us."

Turning to see the man, Thomas backed through the portal.

"Please."

"I can't. I'm sorry." Thomas shut the door. As soon as it was closed, he tried to open it again. The man was in trouble. He had people with him. Thomas had to do the right thing. The door swung open easily.

The room on the other side was missing the back wall and most of the roof had collapsed.

"It's gone," he said.

Did you expect it to still be there? Did the portal you came through stick around?

Thomas slammed the door closed. He heard more of the ceiling collapse on the other side.

What now?

"I keep checking."

TWENTY-SEVEN
Options

Thomas tried as many doors as he could find before the torch burnt out. He crawled into the buildings on both sides of the one where the portals had been. Ascending a rickety wooden staircase, he hopped from the neighbouring roof to the crumbling one to make sure there were no hidden doors in what remained of the attic.

He dug around in the attic for something that looked like it would light on fire. He wished that he had taken some of the ratty clothing that he found in the fancy hotel, but managed to tear strips of tarpaper from the collapsed roof and knotted them around the end of the torch. It took a while to ignite but burned brightly, sending out plumes of dark smoke that he tried to not breathe in.

Are you sure that is a smart idea? the shadow asked.

"I need to see." Thomas held the torch as far out

as he could. The weather-beaten paper curled away and fell to ash. What was left stuck to the wood and glowed a deep orange.

Thomas had to hold the stick close to whatever he wanted to see, but it was better than being in the dark.

Before leaving the crumbling structure, Thomas tried for the third time to open the doors that had led to portals, though there was nothing there. The gem around his neck remained dull yellow.

What will you do now? Go back to the capital and face the zealots?

Shaking his head, Thomas walked deeper into the Wall, squeezing through narrow alleys littered with rubble and climbing over piles of brick and ice.

It would be nearly as dangerous to search blindly for Teacup and her tribe. Do you remember the way back?

"I'm not going there either." Thomas stopped at an archway. It connected a building with huge limestone blocks making up its foundation and the remains of a tall, red-brick apartment. The facade of the apartment building was gone and Thomas could see the tiny rooms inside like an oversized dollhouse.

Holding the torch up to the arch, he made out the carved words. *Cellar Access.*

The walls on either side, though made of different materials, were equally imposing. He walked between them and looked up at the sliver of star-strewn sky overhead.

At the end of the corridor were a set of stairs leading down.

You are not going deeper into the Wall. Archon told you how foolish that would be.

"I am." Thomas leaned into the angled hole, checking the condition of the stairs with what light the torch threw off.

Leave me here. I will not be taken down there.

"I'm sorry." Thomas took the first step downward. "I won't survive without the robe."

You will not survive at all in the depths.

"Something tells me this is my best option." Thomas continued to descend, the stairwell swallowing him as he got beneath the height of the frozen ground. "The cold will kill me. Or starvation will. Or a cannibal."

Or some creature in the dark.

Thomas could feel the gem under the robe. It pushed against his sternum. There was no internal warmth, but it reassured him. "If there were some portals here, there may be more."

And you will go through the next one you find?

"If it's better than here."

Not a difficult achievement.

Thomas stopped. The stairs continued below him, but the opening at the top looked like a window in a dark room. "You don't say anything when other people are around, but when I'm alone, you have opinions on everything."

I know when it is wise to be silent.

Sighing, Thomas turned away from the square of sky and continued to descend deeper. "Could have fooled me."

I am not as fond of you when you are being snarky. You are much more pleasant when you are kowtowing to the will of others.

"I don't know what that means." Thomas put his hand against the wall to hold the waning torch farther in front of him. "Not that I'm asking."

Have you ever heard of the Milgram experiments? I suppose not.

Thomas didn't answer. The glow at the end of the torch dimmed so he held it close to his face and blew gently across it. With each breath, the light intensified briefly before fading.

Find something to stoke that fire or turn around and go back up like a sensible boy.

Thomas kept the embers going until he reached the end of the stairs. The concrete walls were damp and the steady sound of echoing drips fell from the ceiling. Puddles collected in low spots on the uneven floor.

His hand still running along the wall, Thomas felt a damp fuzzy patch and pulled back. He wiped his hand on the robe and shuffled forward.

The floor angled down slightly. Thomas could only tell because a small stream of water ran down the middle, collecting into a miniature lake when it met carpet.

Hopping over the water, Thomas tiptoed across the carpet, each step squishing. He grimaced and blew on the waning torch. The hallway turned and went down again. The stairs doubled back on themselves over and over.

Thomas lost his footing at a gap in the staircase and tumbled until he reached the next landing. The torch bumped his cheek and the spot burned. His ankle and shoulder hurt too. After a moment to wallow in his minor injuries, he got to his feet and continued down the long staircase.

Snow from a Distant Sky

TWENTY-EIGHT
Locked

Thomas made his way down three more sets of stairs before the torch went out completely. The last set were narrow, uneven steps carved out of the surrounding rock. He took his time, not wanting to slip in the water that cascaded past his feet, and fall over the open side.

At the bottom, he heard the loud sound of dripping that echoed over itself, hiding its source. He guessed he was in a natural cave, but had no way to tell. The air was still and cool, but much warmer than outside. Thomas rolled up the sleeves of the robe. The lower half of the fabric was soaked and he had to keep unsticking it from his legs. He stared into the darkness.

What now?

Thomas had no way of telling if the shadow had manifested itself or if it was in the robe. He scratched his head and wished he could take a long, hot shower. "I don't know."

You could go back the way you came. It will take a while, but you should be able to feel your way out.

Shaking his head, Thomas sat on the wet steps. He felt around in the bag and found more dried meat. He guessed that he could last a few days with what he had, if he pushed himself. Though, he would need a source of clean water.

He munched on the ration and weighed his options. He thought about cutting up the bag and using it to burn, but he was hesitant to lose the advantage of having the satchel. Digging out a bottle, he shook it to get a sense of how much water he had left.

I really think you should consider leaving this place. You have been lucky to not run into any creatures or anomalies.

"Don't we need an anomaly?" Thomas stood and tucked the bottle back in the bag. Tapping the floor with his feet, he followed the stream of water flowing from the stairs, using the splashing of his steps as a guide.

He explored the ground ahead of him with his lead foot. He had no way of telling how big the cave was, but he couldn't touch the walls on either side of him.

Thomas shuffled forward for what felt like an hour before his foot touched a ledge. Getting down to his hands and knees, he reached over the edge, feeling for solid ground. If there was a place for him to drop down to, it was out of reach. As far as he was concerned, the ledge was the end of the world.

He crawled along the cliff, periodically feeling over the side.

There were occasional protrusions that he thought he could use as handholds, but he couldn't build up the nerve to climb over the edge.

The cliff curved to the left and he followed it until he met a wall. He felt along the wall for a bit in case there was a way around it, but it was solid. Letting his shoulder slump, he sat against it, a foot over the edge of the cliff.

Thomas kept his eyes closed. He was tired, and it was so dark, he couldn't see anyway. Colours and shapes swirled behind his eyelids, but there was one point of light that didn't move. Reaching for his neck, he felt the chain and pulled the gem out from under the robe.

He opened his eyes and saw the faint glow coming from inside the yellow jewel. When he held it close, the light faded. When he extended his arm as far as he could reach, it got brighter.

"There's something here," he said.

That may be, but it is over the edge you have been skirting.

Thomas got to his feet and leaned out over the cliff. The gem pulsed faintly. He got to his knees and held the gem down along the rock face. It dimmed, but he could make out the facade. He put the necklace back on.

"It's straight out. Over the edge." Thomas felt around the ground and collected a few pebbles.

Too bad you cannot reach it.

"Uh, huh." Thomas tossed one of the pebbles straight out in front of him. It struck something and bounced a few times. He tried the experiment again, throwing lower. The sound of impact rebounded back at him. The third time, he threw higher and after a moment heard the pebble land.

He kept throwing until he was out of ammunition, but he had an idea that there was an opposite cliff and it wasn't too far away. Backing up, his stride extra long, he counted his steps.

If you are giving up, I would appreciate it if you left me here. I will most likely perish before I am found again, but it would be preferable to being on your crumpled body at the bottom of this crevice.

"I'm not giving up yet. Remember when I jumped off the roof?"

Vividly.

Thomas rolled his sore shoulder and took off. At twenty steps, he jumped. In midair, the darkness only broken by the gem hanging from his neck, he felt untethered from the world. He had the sensation of flying just before landing hard. His ankle twisted and he fell face first onto the hard rock.

His lip was split and warmth ran from his nose. The spot where he'd burned his cheek flared on impact, and he was sure he'd cut open his elbow. But, he was on solid ground. Sitting upright, he held the gem in front of his face. He couldn't tell if it was brighter, but there was a subtle pulsing deep inside it.

To be sure he was on the other side of the chasm, or tiny ditch, he backtracked to the cliff. The wall was on his right side and he leaned against it.

"I did it."

So it seems. Was it worth it?

Thomas felt his heart beating hard. He breathed rapidly, pumped full of adrenaline from his blind jump. "I hope so."

He turned around and followed the wall, tapping ahead with his foot. Using the intensity of the pulsing gem as a compass, he found a corridor with smooth walls.

The light of the gem was almost enough to navigate by in the smaller space, but Thomas kept his pace slow, testing his footing with each step.

The hallway ended at a huge round door. It was as tall as Thomas if he stood on his tiptoes and reached up with his fingertips.

The gem flashed like an aircraft-warning beacon. Thomas grabbed the handle, which was as big as his forearm, and pulled, but the door didn't budge.

It is locked. the shadow said.

"I can tell." Thomas put a foot on the frame and pulled as hard as he could, but his shoulder gave out. He groaned and spat blood. His nose had stopped bleeding, but his ankle and elbow throbbed. "There's something on the other side."

That does not mean it is something good.

"I'm not giving up now." Thomas scratched the back of his head and stared at the door in the blinking yellow light.

Curiosity killed the cat.

"I've heard that one." Thomas pushed against the door, but it was as solid as when he pulled. "Didn't satisfaction bring it back?"

A silly rhyme.

Thomas slumped to the ground. "I'm tired."

You have been up for a long time. You should rest. Perhaps a solution will present itself by the time you wake. Or, perhaps something will come along and eat you. Then you will have nothing to worry about.

Covering a yawn, Thomas gripped the gem tightly, blocking most of the light. "Maybe." He closed his eyes and leaned back against the door. "Just for a minute."

TWENTY-NINE
Traveller

There was a loud click that Thomas could feel through his whole body and he was pushed forward. The gem faded in and out regularly, but it was the only source of light in the cave under the Wall.

Thomas rolled onto his knees and rubbed his eyes. "How long was I asleep?"

My apologies. I inadvertently cut your rest to just over three hours. While you slept, I took it upon myself to attempt to connect with the security circuitry in the door. I successfully persuaded it to open.

Yawning, Thomas stood. "You talk too fancy in the morning."

I jimmied the lock. Is that better?

"I don't know about better, but it's less pretentious." Thomas bumped into the open door as he tried to orient himself. It rocked slightly. "Wait. Did you say you got the door open?"

I did tell you I was an artificial intelligence. The room on the other side is a lab. Thankfully, you move a lot more than the wizard who previously wore this robe did. I was able to transfer a little energy and interface with the lock.

"I'm impressed. Thanks." Thomas pulled on the huge door, but his sore shoulder protested. Wedging himself in the narrow opening, he managed to squeeze behind it.

Our lots are unified for the moment.

The gem continued to blink at the same rate. In the yellow gleam, Thomas saw a long metal table with tools and equipment strewn across it. He didn't know what several of the devices were, but the microscope, screwdriver, and multimeter looked like they could have come from his world. Picking up the screwdriver, he blew the layer of dust off of it. "It looks like they left in a hurry."

Or they did not know they would not be returning.

"I guess." Thomas stuffed the screwdriver into his bag as he walked down the long table. He had to step over the broken equipment that had fallen to the floor. Stopping at the end, he grabbed what looked like a watch or fitness tracker with a big rectangular screen that curved around a wrist. "This a smartwatch?"

Oh. An auspicious find. I would not call it smart, but it is a watch with which I can connect. It has some functions as a computer on its own, but the smarts will be provided by me.

Thomas put it on, the rubber strap stretching over his hand. He pressed the single button on the side, but the device remained dark. "Do I have to hold the button?"

It needs time to charge. Your movements should suffice, though I believe this model is also solar.

"Cool." Thomas shook his wrist, but stopped when he felt a twinge of pain. "I don't suppose you know what this lab was for?"

Given that the blinking of your gem led us here, I would hazard a guess that it had something to do with portals. Though, that could be a coincidence.

"Strange place for a lab." Turning around, Thomas looked over what he could see in the flashing light.

When the cataclysm happened, the earth shook for days. The resulting quakes that continued for years were enough to take down buildings. This place may not have always been like this.

"I guess. But, what do I do now?" Nudging a dented metal box with his foot, Thomas sighed.

You followed that gem here. You even made a leap of faith because of it.

"Okay." Nodding, Thomas took off the necklace and held it out in front of him. He spun in a slow circle, staring at the pulsing light. When he was facing a dark corner, the jewel flashed slightly faster.

He walked forward slowly, making sure to not

trip over damaged equipment.

A large, arched shape came into view and the gem flashed quicker. When he was close enough, he moved the gem over the object as if he were holding a lantern.

The arch rose up from a thick, round base with layers of perforated metal overlapping to make the surface. The top of the object was a little over his head and thick cables ran from the peak of the curve back towards the rest of the room along both walls. The whole thing was bolted to the floor with nuts the size of his hand.

"You think this is where the portals come from?" Thomas crouched to get a closer look at the base.

It could be.

"Is there any information in the computer?"

I have no doubt that there is, but I cannot supply enough power to find out.

Thomas stood and backed away from the arch. He tripped on a bundle of wires and stumbled into the long metal table. It shook and items that had survived earthquakes fell.

Instinctively, Thomas put the necklace back on and picked up what had dropped to the floor, likely retrieving more things than he knocked down. One of the items was an old binder. Some of the pages were hanging on to the rings by a single punched hole.

Thomas flipped it open and skimmed the contents in the intermittent yellow light. The text was technical and dense, interspersed with diagrams and charts. He didn't understand most of it, but he did notice written notes in the margins.

The fat, rounded script was as hard to decipher as the technobabble. He picked out words he could read and filled the gaps with context. Most of the notes were about the specific experiments described on the pages where they were written. How one test failed because another scientist wasn't willing to turn up the power, or that the frequency was off and other people's math was unreliable.

Thomas put down the binder and searched the table for others. Eventually, he found a stack of them on a shelf near the huge, round door. Most of the binders were filled with more technical information and few of them had any notes. The ones that did were similarly derisive towards scientists other than the author. At the bottom of the stack, though, he found a smaller binder that looked like someone's personal notebook. It was filled with the same handwriting, but instead of complaints, there were passages about the origin of the experiment. Tucked into the front cover was a pencil and a pen.

"I think this is it." Thomas scanned the pages, looking for something about the portals.

What are you referring to?

"Information about the experiment. What they were doing here." Thomas followed the words with his finger as he read. "Here. It says they were looking for a way to recreate an unexplained phenomenon. Rifts in the fabric of space-time. They thought they could open the rifts wider and..."

And what?

"Uh, it's a little hard to read. It definitely says travel." Flipping through more pages, Thomas stopped when he saw the word rift again. "Here. The rifts were discovered in the Wall, but they don't know where they came from. There are stories of similar distortions in myth, but nothing substantiated." Thomas scratched his head. He was warm in the robe and beads of sweat collected on his hairline. "Okay, they don't know where the portals lead. Maybe to another world or maybe to another time. Or both." Letting the book drop to his side, Thomas went back to the arch. "So, maybe if we can get this machine to work, we can make a portal. And if we can make a portal, maybe we can control where it goes."

We will need to find a way to power it.

Thomas sighed. "Yeah."

You could try seeing where those cables go.

"Oh, yeah. Good point." Thomas stuck the little binder in his pocket with the notebook and followed one of the cables to a wall. The cable disappeared through a hole. He backtracked to the machine and to the opposite corner of the room. The cable went through the wall like the first cable had, but beneath it was a door.

Thomas tried the handle, but it was locked. Rather than find the key, he picked up the heavy remains of a microscope and smashed it down on the handle. The knob broke off and he was able to reach inside the mechanism and unlatch the door.

On the other side was a small room filled with wires running to circuit boxes and a big mainframe taking up an entire wall. Thomas opened the panels and checked the circuits, but none of them were tripped. Examining the mainframe, he noticed a big red switch on the wall. He flipped it upward and sparks shot out of one of the circuit boxes.

He could smell burning plastic, but something inside the metal mainframe whirred to life. Darting back into the lab, he saw electricity arcing from the overhead cable to the metal shelf on the wall. He raced to the arch.

"Any idea where this power is coming from?" Thomas covered his face with his arm as the electricity reached the arch and jumped to the base.

This lab must be connected to some redundant source. A nuclear plant whose automated shutdown has not been tripped or a hydro station still spinning. Any system would be unstable and this intense draw of power could cause it to collapse.

"So, we won't have juice for long?" Thomas looked for a control panel for the device. "How do we choose a destination?"

You should have thought of that before flipping the switch.

A jagged line of light formed in the middle of the arch and shimmered in the same way as the first portal Thomas had seen. The gem around his neck glowed steadily.

Thomas looked over his shoulder to the vault door then back to the forming portal. "I guess it's now or never. What do you want to do?"

That is not much of a choice. Die here alone or be dragged to who knows where.

"I'd be sad to leave you behind." A bolt of electricity flashed past Thomas and hit the metal table, leaving a burn mark. "If I survive."

Going through this portal is a gamble. The chances of it leading to your world are negligible.

"The chances of me finding another one here before I freeze to death aren't so great either." Thomas stepped closer to the arch. Through the portal, he could make out the hazy view of a coastline with rocky cliffs off in the distance.

There was an explosion in the electrical room and the power faded for an instant. Smoke drifted into the lab, curling up to the ceiling. "I'm going,"

Thomas yelled over the crackling of electricity.

I suppose you will need my help wherever you end up.

"So, you're coming with me?"

Yes, yes. Get on with it.

Clasping the gem in one hand and gripping the cuff of the robe in the other, Thomas walked forward into the arch and through the portal.

Snow from a Distant Sky

EPILOGUE
On the Other Side

The single sun blazed low over the rising tide. It looked so big that Thomas would have believed that it was going to drop right into the ocean and be extinguished for the night.

He stood as still as he could in the shallows. The waves, getting higher by the minute, broke against his knees, then his thighs. A brightly coloured fish swam nearby. Thomas didn't know what kind it was, or if it was found in his world. He'd hesitated when he cooked and ate the first one he'd caught, not knowing if the bright green and red stripes over the pale body was a warning that it was toxic or just random beauty.

At the next big wave, the fish darted between Thomas' legs. He plunged his hands into the water and snatched it, managing to avoid the sharp spines on the dorsal fins along its back.

It wriggled in his grasp, but he'd been catching them for weeks and had managed to find the perfect amount of force to use to keep hold of it while not squeezing too hard and rocketing it away like a wet bar of soap.

The fish was a little bigger than soap. He carried it out of the water and to the roaring fire on the beach. Following the shadow's directions, Thomas had made a rack that hung over the fire so he could smoke the fish, preserving them longer than just cooking them.

Thomas bashed the fish on a rock and split it open across the belly with his knife. He was getting better with the flaying, but it took time. Setting the fresh fish on the rack to smoke with the others, he went back to the rising water to wash off his hands.

The watch around his wrist vibrated. A message icon flashed on the curved screen.

He tapped it and text scrolled around his wrist.

Do you have enough provisions yet?

Thomas stripped off his wet underwear as he made his way back to the fire. On the opposite side of the drying rack was a palm tree bent so far over that he could sit on it like a bench. Laying the underwear across the trunk, he slipped on his shorts and sat next to the robe.

The thin, rough fabric danced in the constant breeze.

Well? it wrote.

"When this batch is done in the morning, we can go. We'll follow the stream all the way to the mountain." Thomas picked up his bottle and took a long drink.

I must say, you have grown more confident this last month in this new world.

"Well." Thomas looked behind him. "So far nothing scary has crashed out of the tree line and I'm not at risk of freezing to death every night,"

Getting to his feet, Thomas took hold of the necklace. The yellow gem caught the setting sun but beyond the red and orange gleam was a faint yellow pulse. He held it towards the mountain that loomed over the beach and the light grew slightly.

Storm clouds swirled over the peak all day and night, as long as he'd been in the world.

The notebook he'd taken from the lab had a section on the beach. It was the only portal the scientists had managed to open and while none of them had gone through it, they had sent probes over.

"As far as we know, that storm has been going for decades." Thomas scratched his belly. "I'm not in a hurry to experience it up close."

How long do you think you can survive here on this beach? Besides, do you not want to get home?

"Yeah, yeah," Thomas grabbed a fish off the rack and took a bite. Spitting out the bones, he wiped the juice from his chin. "Like I said. Tomorrow."

THAT'S ALL FOR NOW...
SEE YOU SOON
ON ANOTHER
WORLD!

Acknowledgements

The entire time I was writing and editing this story, I was preoccupied with it being the last book in the series (I hope only for now). Throughout the series, I've had tremendous help and support from a group of amazing and diverse people. I can't thank them enough for all their support and encouragement. And their honest criticism.

Once again, I relied on Christian Laforet as my first reader. We haven't been able to write in person for two years, but I can count on him to know what I mean and point out when things aren't clear. That, and he's been aware the basic concept from the first book. I hope I managed to stick the landing after years of hyping it up.

As my biggest supporters for the longest time, I'm happy I was able to get my parents' opinions on the early drafts. The balance of support will always tip in their favour. They're always there for me in little ways and big ones, and I'm continuously grateful to them.

My brother kept me excited through the long days of writing alone in my room. His enthusiasm and unique perspective, as well as his understanding of my humour, is a big part of why I can share these books with others.

I dedicated this book to the Writing Wrecking Crew. We haven't been able to meet in person for a while, but I know they're out there working hard. They ask important questions and are eager to come to my aid when I need knowledgeable opinions. Writing is a solo adventure, but it's a lot more fun with friends at your side.

No book gets to the end without dedicated beta readers. Sephorah Phojola, Brittni Brinn, Justin Cantelo, James Martin, Cynthia Ing, and Natalie Carbert all took the time to read the early drafts, search for typos, and make suggestions. They helped me shape the book and clean up the rough edges. Any remaining mistakes are my own fault.

The enigmatic C.M. Forest wrote an overwhelmingly positive quote for the back cover. I was a little hesitant to print it as he wrote it, but he insisted the book was worth the praise. I just wish I knew who he really was.

I was lucky enough to once again convince Glen Hawkes to design the cover image for this book. I knew what I wanted this book to look like and he not only took that idea and brought it into the real world, he made it better than the picture in my head. He's obviously talented, but he's also one of the best collaborators I've worked with.

Ben Van Dongen was born in Windsor Ontario. He likes to think that if he tried harder he could have been an Astronaut, but he is happier writing science fiction anyway. He wrote the Synthetic Albatross Novella Series, co-authored the book No Light Tomorrow, and is one half of the founding team of Adventure Worlds Press. You can read more crazy notions on his website. **BenVanDongen.com**

Photo by Khoa Nguyen

More Books by the Author

The Synthetic Albatross Series

The Earth Books
The Thinking Machine
The Neon Heart
Break/Interrupt

The Offworld Books
Broadcast Wasteland
Snow from a Distant Sky

Anthologies
No Light Tomorrow